SUMMIT OF PASSION

ELENA AITKEN

Ink Blot Communications

Chapter One

MAYBE THERE WOULD BE a medical emergency? Maybe, if she got lucky, someone would have a heart attack and she'd be called down to town. Deanna Gordon shook her head and mentally scolded herself. No. That wasn't okay. It was never okay to wish someone ill health. Even if it would be a good excuse to get her off the ski hill and away from Marcus Stone, who currently walked toward her, his snowboard casually hefted over his shoulder and looking so damn sexy that it interfered with Deanna's ability to think straight.

If she could just think of something—*anything*—to get out of the afternoon snowboarding lesson from Marcus. She just couldn't seem to make her brain work fast enough to come up with a plausible explanation for blowing off the very generous gift from Seth McBride and her old friend Cynthia Giles. Ever since she returned to Cedar Springs about a month ago, she'd been their doctor and had been the one to officially declare Cynthia pregnant. Being able to see one of her oldest friends through such a special experience was definitely one of the perks of being a doctor in her hometown. It may be the only perk that she could think of. And there were definitely drawbacks, and the biggest one stood in front of her with a killer smile and a look in his eyes that had never before failed to make her stomach flip.

"Ready to do this?"

It was too late. She couldn't think of a damn thing to say to get her out of it. Not without looking like a total bitch, anyway. "Absolutely." She gave him her sweetest smile. Maybe if she faked her way through the afternoon, it would go faster. Besides, if she remembered correctly, she wasn't the only one who was affected by spending time in close proximity together. The way she remembered it, their connection had been very much a mutual thing.

"You got a rental board?" Marcus bent down to pick up her snowboard from where it rested at her feet. "What happened to yours?"

"How do you know it's not mine?"

"Your board used to have those big pink flowers all over it." He smiled when he spoke, and damned if it didn't send thrills right through her. She wasn't supposed to be so affected by him.

"That was years ago." She grabbed the board from him. "How do you remember that?"

"I remember a lot of things."

His words were laced with the memories of long ago, and judging by the intensity of his eyes, those memories were just as real for him as they were for her. Only she wasn't naive enough to think that Marcus had spent any of the two years since they'd last seen each other lying in bed, staring up at the ceiling, and remembering exactly what it felt to lie together and feel the heat from his body wrapped around her. Not that she had. Not in months, anyway. And there was no way he needed to know that.

"Well, I hope I remember how to snowboard." She put as much flippancy into her voice as she could manage. Deanna was determined to keep the situation as light as possible. There was no need to bring any feelings or memories into play. In fact, it was probably for the best if she could just repress all of those feelings. No. It was *definitely* for the best.

"I'm sure it'll all come back to you." Marcus dropped his board to the snow and stepped in. "And there's only one way to find out." He strapped his boot into the binding, and Deanna followed suit. There was no point prolonging the torture. Besides, the sooner she got it over with, the better. "Ready?" he asked after a moment and Deanna simply nodded.

Thankfully, they were joined on the chairlift by two skiers who were visiting on a ski holiday and with it being their first trip to Stone Summit, they had plenty of questions to keep Marcus busy for the ride up the mountain. Despite the fact that she was saved from making conversation with him, Deanna was distinctly aware of his strong thigh pressed up against hers and she could feel the heat even through her thick snow pants.

"Ready for this?" Marcus looked over at her as they approached the top of the chairlift; she nodded and bit down on her bottom lip. Getting off the chair was always her least favorite part. She'd fallen one time and caused a bit of a jam-up of people, and although it had only happened once, the whole situation had been so mortifying, she always got nervous when it came to disembark. No matter how many times she'd done it successfully. "You'll be fine." He put his hand on her leg.

It was so unexpected, Deanna jerked her head up and stared at him right as their boards hit the snow-covered ramp at the top of the lift. Before she knew what was happening, Marcus took her hand to guide her off the chair and down the ramp. The entire time her board slid beneath her, all she could think of was that Marcus was touching her, and how nothing good could come from it.

THE HEAT FROM HER HAND, even through the thick glove, singed Marcus to the core. It had been two and a half years. Long enough that the woman shouldn't have that kind of effect on him. He took a second to compose himself, thankful that Deanna wasn't looking at him. After he'd let go of her hand, she'd sat in the snow and had focused on strapping her boot into the board ever since. She definitely gave it more attention than was necessary, but he wasn't going to say anything; he needed the time to pull himself together. He knew it was a bad idea to take Deanna Gordon out snowboarding. No, it was flat out a bad idea for him to be alone with her in any capacity. And even if it didn't make any sense, and even if he knew logically that those old feelings should have burned out long ago, it was clear they hadn't. Hell, he'd only held her hand, and through a glove nonetheless. His body should not react the way it was. He shouldn't have the intense urge to grab her and pull her tight to him so she could feel for herself that his body still remembered hers.

But he couldn't. He'd lost that right a long time ago. Not that he'd even had it. Not really.

Marcus dropped down next to her in the snow and strapped his own boot into his board. "Okay." He straightened up. "Are you ready to do this?" He knew his face was a carefully composed mask. He wouldn't give anything away.

She nodded.

"Let's start on an easy run, just until it comes back to you. Sound good?"

She nodded again.

"So remember, just point your board down and relax your body. I think you'll be surprised with how much it remembers." She still didn't say anything, but nodded her agreement. "Are you good, Dee?" He slipped easily into the use of her nickname. "You're not saying much."

She looked away and stared down over the hill. "I'm good. I got this."

He smiled and resisted the urge to reach out and touch her again. She'd always been so determined. It was one of the things that had attracted him to her in the first place. He'd never seen such a driven woman. When she set her mind to something, she went after it. It had been hot as hell back then, when she had just graduated from medical school and was home for a break, and it was even hotter now. "Then let's do this." He pushed up off the snow.

Because he was the teacher, he waited until Deanna headed down the hill. He watched as she started off shaky and unsure but in only a few turns, she settled in and carved through the snow as if it had only been a few days instead of years since she'd been on a board. He grinned and with a jump, set off down the mountain to catch up with her.

They finished the easy run with no drama and when Deanna pulled the goggles off her face onto her helmet, her broad, beautiful smile took over her face. "That was amazing. I totally remembered how to do it."

Marcus laughed. "Of course you did. Once a boarder, always a boarder. And the next one's going to be even better."

"Next one? Are we doing it again?" She clapped her gloved hands like a little girl.

"Of course. This lesson isn't over yet." He bent and freed one foot from the board and she did the same. When he stood again, he watched her for a second.

"Are you ready?" Deanna swung her head around and caught him staring at her. "What?"

He shook his head. "Nothing. Should we go?" He'd made himself vulnerable to her once before and she'd broken his heart. He'd be dammed if he was going to let it happen again.

He'd never believed in love at first sight; hell, Marcus had never believed in love. But when he met Deanna, it was instant. Their time together had been short, but it had been intense and the only real feelings he'd ever had for a woman. Not that it mattered; she'd rejected him and completely broken his heart, turning tail and returning to Toronto without so much as a second glance. As if he'd meant nothing to her. And he hadn't been able to say a word about it, because at that time, Marcus hadn't exactly been available to be with another woman, let alone fall in love with one. He'd been dating Kylie Wilson, who now happened to be happily engaged to his twin brother, Malcolm.

He wasn't proud of his past, or the fact that he'd been a terrible boyfriend to Kylie. It wasn't a secret that Marcus had cheated on Kylie—a lot—and generally treated her terribly. That was ancient history, and Kylie had long since forgiven him. But what was a secret was that one of those people he'd cheated on her with had been Deanna. No one in town knew that they'd been together, and he'd hated keeping it a secret, but not nearly as much as Deanna had. He'd known at the time it was killing her to lie to her family and friends, but he'd pushed to keep it quiet until the night he put it all on the line and told her he was in love with her and he wanted to be with her.

He was so sure she'd meet him the next day so together they could go tell Kylie the truth, and finally be free to be together. He'd been up all night planning how they could make things work together: her and her medical career, and him with his dreams to be a professional snowboarder. It seemed impossible, but he knew it wasn't. He'd never felt so full of hope and possibility—he'd been madly in love.

But she never showed up at his apartment the way they'd planned. He'd waited for hours, called her, left messages before he finally discovered she'd left and gone back to Toronto. She never even said good-bye and he was crushed. A few days later, the offer came to join the pro snowboarding circuit, and Marcus had left town, too, vowing never to let himself be so vulnerable again. And he hadn't.

"You look like you're thinking about something," Deanna pushed. "Everything okay?"

Marcus put a smile on his face and gave her a wink. "Perfectly." He pushed his way into the chairlift line.

Whatever had happened between them, it had happened a long time ago in a complete different world and as far as he was concerned, Deanna was just another piece of ass from his past. At least that's what he was going to keep telling himself. At least until he started to believe it.

SHE'D MANAGED to work all her nerves out during the first run, and Deanna was surprised how quickly boarding came back to her. More than that, she was surprised by how much she enjoyed it. The thrill of the cold air on her face as she pushed her body to perform was exhilarating.

"I forgot how awesome this was!" Deanna called behind her as she moved down the hill.

Marcus caught up to her easily and sprayed her with snow as he carved close to her and passed her.

She could only hear his laughter as he went by, and she pushed even harder to catch him although there was no way she could. But Marcus slowed, a move she knew he'd done on purpose, and they finished the run together, coming to a stop in front of the lodge.

"That was fantastic," Deanna said through deep breaths as she tried to control her breathing. "But man, I'm out of shape."

"I think your shape looks pretty fantastic."

She snapped her head up to see his eyes glittering with mischief. After the initial sparks between them—or at least, on her end—she'd managed to compartmentalize any of her left-over feelings for Marcus and enjoy herself despite them. Not that her body wasn't completely aware of his proximity when they rode up the chair together, or when he guided her with a hand on her lower back as they made their way through the line. No, her body was totally aware of him, but the only way she knew to survive being close to Marcus was to bottle up every single one of those feelings, the same way she had years ago. And that's just what she did. So far it had worked pretty well. But that was when she'd had snowboarding to distract her. Now that they stood only inches apart, with no boards between them, Deanna suddenly wasn't so sure how to behave. What was the etiquette for such a situation?

"So," she started, "I guess I should—"

"Hey!"

They both turned at the voice. Deanna's stomach flipped while her heart soared. "Kylie?" She was going to run over to her old friend, but stopped herself only seconds before she remembered her boots were still strapped into the board. She quickly bent and released herself but by the time she had, Kylie had joined them. Deanna wrapped her friend into a bear hug. Catching up through social media and email just wasn't the same and they really hadn't had much time to chat at Kylie's party a few weeks ago—not that Deanna had made the time. She felt guilty about avoiding her, but despite the fact that it had been years since she'd betrayed her by sneaking around with Marcus, and Kylie was now happier than ever with Malcolm, the guilt had only gotten worse. She hated herself for what she'd done all those years ago; it didn't matter that Kylie had never found out. In fact, that little detail probably only made it worse.

"I thought you were gone at nursing school," Deanna said. "What are you doing here?"

Kylie laughed and looked over her shoulder at Malcolm, who just joined them. "Malcolm has an elaborate schedule that gets me back here as much as possible. I swear, it's like I never left."

"Well, I'll take it while we can." Malcolm wrapped his arm around Kylie and pulled her close. "Classes have only just started. Pretty soon my little student here will be too busy studying to come visit me."

Kylie smacked him lightly in the chest. "Stop it. I'll never be too busy for you." She gave him a sweet look that ended in a passionate kiss. Deanna glanced at Marcus, and they exchanged a quick look.

"We have to go have coffee or something," Kylie said to her when she was done smooching her fiancé. "We can steal Cynthia away, too, and get all caught up on everything. I'm so glad you're back in town."

"I'm not really back."

"Well, you're more back than I am these days." Kylie laughed. "Seriously, I feel like going to nursing school came at the worst time ever. With Cynthia's baby and now you being back, it's—"

"The perfect time." Malcolm interrupted her with a smile and a quick kiss on the forehead. "You're going to be the best nurse ever, and there would never be a good time to go away."

"It's true," Marcus chimed in. "Besides, we'll keep Malcolm plenty busy while you're away."

Kylie glanced between the two brothers and shook her head. "That's what I'm afraid of." She looked toward Deanna. "You're going to have to help me out."

"Me?" Deanna's hand flew to her chest. "How can I help you?"

"Keep this one out of trouble," she pointed to Marcus and shook her head, "and far away from my man."

"What?" Deanna took a step back. "Why would I be able to keep him out of trouble?" She didn't dare risk a glance at Marcus, afraid of what simply looking at him would give away. "I don't know any—"

Kylie's laughter cut her off. "You know how he can be."

A completely irrational fear rose up in Deanna. Kylie couldn't possibly know that of course, Deanna knew exactly how Marcus could be because he'd been that way with her. No. She couldn't know, but if she did...Deanna glanced around; the proper words for what should be a completely simple situation totally eluded her.

Ironically, Marcus saved her. "Of course she knows how I can be," he said. "Or should I say, how I used to be. A man can change, Kylie. I'm no longer the troublemaker you seem to think I am." He gave her such a charming smile, even Deanna was fooled by his words.

"You know I love you, Marcus." Kylie beamed at him. "And all that's ancient history. I'm on to bigger and better things these days."

It was much later, after Deanna and Kylie made promises to get together for coffee or drinks, and Deanna had returned her equipment and drove down the mountain to her childhood home, that Kylie's words played on repeat in her head. *That's ancient history.*

Was it? Would Kylie forgive her for betraying her friendship all those years ago when she risked everything to follow her instincts on a love that she'd ultimately walked away from?

Chapter Two

"DEANNA? ARE YOU HOME?"

Deanna shook her head, even though no one could see her on her bed in her pajamas at only eight o'clock, let alone her mother who hollered from the kitchen. And if her mother could see her, she certainly wouldn't be happy with the way Dee was rolling her eyes. Besides that, her mother knew damn well she was home. Where else would she be? It was Cedar Springs, for God's sake. It's not as if she were back in Toronto, where something was going on every night. No, being back in Cedar Springs was definitely a change of pace.

More like a full stop.

With a sigh, she put her Kindle down, which was fine because she'd been reading the same page over and over again on her latest romance novel. Not that it wasn't a good book; it was. In fact, Daire St. Denis was one of her favorite authors. But instead of enjoying her latest sexy story, it only frustrated Deanna. And it definitely served to remind her it had been way too long since she'd been with a man. There may be nonstop activity in Toronto, but who was she kidding? Deanna didn't have time to enjoy any of it. Getting her residency done and building a career definitely hampered a romantic life, never mind a sex life. The most action she got was alone, in the bath.

"Hello? Deanna, are you—"

Deanna opened the door to reveal her mother, who looked as if she was about to open the door regardless of the sign that read, Private: Please Knock. It hadn't worked when she was a teenager and it clearly didn't work now that she was a grown woman. It was a miracle her mother hadn't taken it down. But why would she? Her mother had left her room completely untouched. It was kind of eerie, and at the same time comforting, to sleep in her old room with everything the same. But she could do with a few changes. Specifically, a lock.

She turned her attention to her mother. "Mom? What's up?"

"I'm glad I found you." Her mother smiled, and Deanna couldn't help but return it despite her frustration. She might be sixty-five, but Gayle Gordon was every bit as vibrant and beautiful as when Deanna was a child. Everyone who had ever met her mother couldn't help but be happy in her presence; she simply radiated joy. A detail that had been both a blessing and an annoyance for Deanna growing up. It was hard to be an angst-ridden teenager when your mother was always so cheerful. Which was probably why Deanna had never bothered. It was easier just to smile and be the good girl.

"Hey, Mom. I was just—"

"Sleeping? Don't tell me you were sleeping already? It's barely past eight. Your father and I were just going out."

Seriously? Now her parents had a richer social life than she did? Figures. "Where are you going at this time of night?"

Her mother laughed. "Why don't you come with us, dear?"

Before her mother had even finished asking, Deanna shook her head and backed up. There was no way she was so hard up for a social life that she was going to go out with her parents on a Friday night.

"Why not? Do you have something more pressing to do?" Gayle teased and grabbed Deanna's worn cotton pajama pants. "Besides, we haven't spent any real time with you since you've been home, and your father and I wanted to talk to you about your future."

Oh hell no. The last thing she needed was to get into a discussion about what her mom and dad wanted for her. In fact, if she could get through the next month without having the conversation, and instead focus her energy on finding her father an associate who wasn't her, she could hightail it back to the other side of the country. Her older brother, Dane, had the right idea when it came to escaping small-town life: don't just go to the other side of the country—leave it completely. "Not tonight, Mom."

"Yes, tonight." Her mother pressed her lips together and assessed her. "I know what you're trying to do, but avoiding the situation isn't going to make it go away."

"I'm not—"

"Five minutes. Meet us downstairs."

Deanna watched her, her back straight as a rod as she walked away. As soon as she disappeared around the corner, she leaned up against the doorjamb and sighed. She'd change and she'd go out with her parents because that's what she did. She'd always been the dutiful daughter, doing what was requested of her: get good grades, date the types of guys they approved of, apply to medical school. She'd played the whole *perfect daughter* thing her whole life. Wasn't that the whole reason she found herself back in Cedar Springs, after all?

THE VIEW from his brother's chalet was amazing. Situated right on the ski hill, the house looked out over Stone Summit from the back windows and out the front, the entire valley was spread out in front of him. It was the type of house Marcus had always wanted for himself. Except, it wasn't his. It was his twin brother's. Even though Malcolm hadn't put any kind of time line on Marcus staying there, he knew if he was going to stay in Cedar Springs, he would need to find his own place.

Preferably something as posh as his current digs. Although, even with the money he had saved up from being on the circuit and sponsor endorsements, there was no way he'd be able to afford something comparable.

He returned his attention to his laptop and the real estate ads he'd searched. There wasn't much of a rental market in Cedar Springs, and from the few places that were available, none of them allowed pets.

"I suppose you're going to want to come to, huh, Koda?" Marcus asked the pup, who was currently snuggled in the dog bed with Malcolm and Kylie's puppy, Glade. When Seth and Cynthia's dog, Nala, had puppies, it had been a bit of an impulse for Marcus to claim one of his own, especially considering he wasn't sure where he'd be in the next few months. Sure, he kept telling people he was done with the pro snowboarding circuit and he was trading it in for a life of ski hill maintenance in Cedar Springs, but he was pretty sure even he didn't buy that story. Nobody had asked him outright what his plans were, or why he'd given up the circuit, something he'd dreamed about for years, but Marcus wasn't stupid. There'd be questions soon enough. He'd have to think of something to tell them, because there was no way it would be the truth.

Getting suspended from the circuit was bad enough. But getting suspended because of drugs, when he hadn't even done anything wrong, was too much. No one would believe his side of the story, especially when his coaches hadn't at first. *No.* Testing positive for marijuana in your system was black or white. It didn't matter that Marcus himself had never and would never partake in the drug. But he knew exactly what must have happened. Rich Swanson, the newest kid on the circuit, *had* been partaking. Young and stupid, Rich thought he was untouchable. And apparently he was. He must have friends in high places, too, because Marcus was convinced the tests had been switched.

The circuit had a zero-tolerance policy. No amount was okay. And he'd been placed on immediate suspension. But he'd fought it. Of course he had; he knew he was in the right. Ultimately, the two other boarders who'd tested positive, and legitimately so, had been indefinitely suspended while Marcus's coaches had agreed to a two-month suspension. They, too, struggled with the idea that Marcus would be stupid enough to choose drugs over his career, but they had to do something. All he had to do to get back into the good books was provide a clean blood test. Easy. They'd agreed to keep it quiet from his sponsors, who would drop him like a rock if they heard. It had been over two months but he still hadn't done the test. His pride kept getting in the way. He knew logically it didn't make sense. He had nothing to hide, after all, but they should have taken him at his word.

It may have been his dream job—traveling all over the world, boarding on the best hills, competing and maybe even having a shot at the Olympics in a few years—but now he had a black mark on his record and he wasn't sure yet if he wanted to go back. Something was holding him back. He just didn't know what it was.

Not that he had a lot of other choices. Working for his brother certainly wasn't high on the list. With a groan, Marcus turned back to his screen and kept scrolling. There had to be something available to rent that would take a dog. Or maybe...he looked out over the ski hill that was lit up for night skiing. Maybe he'd just stay put until Malcolm kicked him out. He slammed his laptop shut. It was too much to think about. Besides, the way things were turning out in Cedar Springs these days, he might just have to swallow his pride, take the damn test and go back to the circuit. Because there was no way in hell he would stay in town if Deanna was here. He couldn't get her out of his head and that was definitely not good.

"Come on, puppies, let's get out of here." The huskies hopped up from their bed and eagerly joined Marcus at the door. They may not be very old yet, but they definitely knew enough to know when it looked like they might get to play in the snow.

At almost nine, the night skiers were winding down and the base of Stone Summit was busy with people packing up for the day, heading in for an après ski drink or just generally bustling about. When he'd left the house, he wasn't sure where he was going; all he knew was he needed to get out and get some fresh air to clear his head. Not that it would help. Thoughts of Deanna would still dominate his every waking moment, and he damn well knew it. Because from the moment he saw her at the party a few weeks ago, she'd been on his mind constantly.

It had taken him almost three years to get her out of his head the first time and he'd had to leave town and start a whole new life to do it once. If she was going to stay in Cedar Springs, there was sure as hell no way he'd be there. Sure, he had a lot of self-control and more pride than was healthy for one man, but he also had limits—and coexisting with her in such close proximity definitely pushed those limits. Hard.

He bent and threw a few snowballs for the puppies to chase. They rolled and dove over one another, turning their little game of fetch into a wrestling match the way only puppies could do. Of course, the little fur balls attracted their fair share of attention, and soon enough a group of people clustered around the dogs, oohing and ahhing over how cute they were and asking Marcus questions. He tried to distract himself with a cute little blond who was definitely more interested in him than the dogs, but it didn't work. His heart wasn't in it. Not only was she not Deanna, she didn't even come close to the pull the good doctor had on him. And always had.

It was no secret that he'd been a royal jackass all those years ago when he'd been dating Kylie and cheating on her with every ski bunny who winked at him, but Deanna had been different right from the start and not just because she was a friend of Kylie's. That only made the whole situation even more complicated than it already was. And it was. She'd just graduated from medical school and had come home for the holidays for a quick break before heading into residency. From the moment their eyes met, he was completely lost. It was like something out of a bad eighties romance movie. Only it had been real. For her too.

Deanna had hated lying to Kylie. It ate her up inside and because it hurt her, it hurt Marcus. But despite how wrong they both knew it was, neither of them could do a damn thing about it. Like a magnetic force, they were pulled together over and over again until finally Marcus told her he was in love with her, and the next day, she was gone.

A week later, he'd received a letter in the mail with no return address. All it said was, "I'm sorry."

There was no way he could ask anyone for her address, not without admitting their deception to everyone and he couldn't out Deanna like that. Not when she wasn't around to defend herself or explain things to Kylie. No. So what had he done instead? He'd skipped town himself. Taking the offer for the professional circuit, Marcus left shortly after, and much the same way Deanna had. Without a word to anyone. Not even Kylie.

"Glade. Koda." He called the dogs away from the crowd and walked down one of the back paths through the trees. He thought he'd needed fresh air, but it wasn't enough. He needed to be alone. But that was making him crazy. Hell, he didn't know what he needed. It was happening all over again: the confusion, the uncertainty, the total and complete chaos in his brain. Deanna did that to him. And he'd sworn once that he'd never allow himself to go there again. Fool me once and all that.

"Dammit." He kicked a rock in his path and the dogs scurried off into the trees to fetch it. She was making him crazy, and they'd only spent one afternoon together. "Pull your shit together, Marcus Stone. She's just a girl." *No. She's a woman.* He shook his head in a futile effort to clear it. Dammit, he was arguing with himself now. This had to stop. He needed to get her out of his head once and for all.

Too bad the only way he could think of to accomplish that was by having her one last time. Just like the cure to having a song stuck in your head on repeat was to listen to the song, maybe the only way to get Deanna Gordon out of his head was to have her curvy, luscious body beneath his, her dark eyes blazing with passion and her nails digging into his back as she screamed out his name. Hell, he didn't know if that was the way to cure himself of her, but judging by the way his cock twitched in his pants, it was the best damn idea he'd had all day.

WHEN HER PARENTS had more or less forcibly dragged her out of the house, Deanna had expected they would take her for a nice dinner. Maybe to the Stillwater, up at the Springs resort. Or if they didn't want to have something quite so fancy, maybe even Peppi's, the new pizza place that had just opened up on Main Street. Sure, there weren't a lot of options in Cedar Springs, but Deanna would have guessed at least half a dozen places before she would have guessed they'd take her to the Grizzly Paw. The Paw was the local pub, and despite the fact that it was usually packed now with skiers and weekend tourists, it was also the most popular hangout for the locals. The locals under the age of sixty, that was.

"The Paw?" She'd questioned from the backseat of his car, as they pulled up in front of the pub. "Wouldn't you rather go somewhere else?"

"Don't be silly," her father, Jim, said. "The Paw has the five-dollar draft for locals on the weekends. Besides that, your mother likes Archer's chicken wings."

"His wings?" Deanna shook her head, resolved to the fact that she would be walking into the local pub with her parents, who clearly had more of a life than she did.

Her mother stood on the sidewalk and adjusted her scarf. "Oh, Jim. You do know I love those chicken wings. I'm not sure what Archer does to them," she continued, as if the wings were a fine delicacy. "But he makes them so crispy and the sauce coats them just so."

"He deep-fries them, Mom." Deanna walked with her up the stairs and held the door open for her parents. "They're fried in oil and they're really not good for you."

"Nonsense." Gayle waved her hand in her daughter's direction and swept past her into the pub. "I'm pretty sure he bakes them," she called over her shoulder.

There was no point arguing with her, and Deanna only shook her head and followed her parents into the pub where she probably should have been anyway. The building was packed with a combination of faces she recognized and those she didn't. Either they were new to town, or they were visiting. Either way, Deanna wasn't too worried about it. Besides a few of her best friends, she wasn't very interested in fostering any friendships in Cedar Springs because she certainly didn't intend to stay. It was harsh, and a somewhat anti-social way to look at things, but it was the truth and as far as Deanna was concerned, there was no point pussyfooting around the truth.

Moments after they settled into a booth, Samantha

Harrison—or Burke, as Deanna knew her—arrived with menus and a quick wipe of the table.

"Deanna! It's so good to see you." Sam slid paper coasters onto the table as she spoke. "What's it been? Two years?"

"Almost three."

"We've been trying," Gayle jumped in. "But we just couldn't seem to get her to come back home."

"Until now, that is." Her father grinned. "It's good to have her back."

"For a visit," Deanna clarified. She turned to Sam. "I'm only here helping out for a bit." She shot a glare in her parents' direction. It didn't seem to matter how many times she told them; they would not accept the fact that Deanna wasn't staying.

Obviously sensing some tension, Sam let them know the specials, took their drink orders and disappeared.

"That girl works so hard," Deanna's mother said the moment Sam was gone. "She's been running herself ragged with this place and managing everything, along with a new husband. It's a wonder how she does it all. And if she's going to have babies one day, she might want to consider getting a little more help. It's not easy to have a family."

Deanna tried not to roll her eyes. Her mother's views on marriage were extremely traditional; hell, her mother's views on pretty much everything were traditional. And although she knew her mother was proud of the fact that she'd become a doctor, Deanna was fairly sure she would have been much happier if Deanna had just settled down with a nice, successful man and raised a family. The successful part being a crucial component.

"I'm sure she loves what she does, Mom."

"Isn't it nice to see all you girls back in town doing what you love?"

Deanna turned to stare at her father. She knew exactly what he was trying to do, and she wasn't going to buy into it.

"It's nice to be *visiting*, Dad." She smiled sweetly. "But remember, this is only temporary until I can help you find an associate." Her dad nodded, but she knew he still hadn't heard her. Not really. "It's temporary, Dad. I'm not staying."

"Oh Deanna. You don't have to be so dramatic," her mother said. "We know you don't want to live here, although I don't understand that. Cedar Springs is a perfectly nice place to raise a family."

"What family?"

"Well, not now." Her mother smiled and turned to accept her drink as Samantha returned with a full tray. "But one day, certainly. You're not getting any younger, Deanna. Maybe it's time to find a nice man and settle down."

Deanna tried not to choke as she took a sip of the drink Sam had just handed her. She sputtered and coughed before she managed to speak. "Are you kidding?"

"Not at all." Gayle smiled innocently. "You tell her, Samantha. Don't you think Cedar Springs is just the perfect place to settle down and have a family?"

A dark look crossed Sam's face briefly, but it was gone a second later. "I certainly like it," she said tentatively.

Deanna crossed her arms on the table. If her mother really felt like having this particular conversation at this moment, so be it. "But there would have to be men in town worth settling down with," she said. "And if you haven't noticed, Cedar Springs is a really small town. There aren't really a lot of men."

"Samantha found one," her mother said, dragging Sam into the conversation. "There's no reason you can't find one, too."

"Trent Harrison isn't from here, Mom. Besides, from what I can tell, all of the good ones are taken." Deanna got ready to play her trump card. "If you want me to settle down with a nice, respectable man and give you grandchildren one day, I'm going to have to look somewhere besides Cedar Springs."

Samantha stifled a giggle at Gayle's look when she realized Deanna may have made a solid point. "Let me take your order," Sam said, no doubt anxious to get herself out of the conversation.

After she left again, it was Deanna's father who took over the conversation. "I know you think you don't want to practice in Cedar Springs."

"I don't think, Dad. I know."

"Hear me out."

She smiled and nodded for her dad to continue. "But I do appreciate your commitment to helping me out until we can find someone who does want the practice."

"I said I would." And she'd kicked herself ever since. When her dad had called to ask her to help him out in Cedar Springs, she hadn't considered how difficult it would be to find someone who wanted a small town life. It was a much lower salary than a big city doctor could command and of course it also meant longer hours, on-call shifts at the hospital, and the sometimes tedium of small-town problems without all the excitement of a big city emergency room. So far, the advertisements she'd placed hadn't garnered much interest, her father certainly hadn't helped with the search, and it looked more and more like she'd be in Cedar Springs longer than originally planned.

"Well, we do appreciate it, kiddo." He reached out and squeezed Deanna's hand. She'd always been a daddy's girl; heck, she'd even followed in his footsteps. He was definitely her weak spot. Deanna would do anything to make her father happy. Even if it meant putting her own life in Toronto on hold. *Not that there'd been much of a life there lately.* Nothing real anyway.

"I know you do, Dad."

"And maybe while you're here you'll be able to find a man, too."

"Mom. Seriously."

Her mother shrugged but Deanna didn't fall for the innocent act. "I'm just saying, it's been nice to watch your old friends settle down with nice young men. Cynthia and the McBride boy. Who would have thought that would be a love match?"

"Who would've thought?" Deanna mumbled.

"And Kylie." Her mother beamed. "I can't tell you how happy it makes me to see Kylie with the right Stone brother after all this time. Their wedding will be—"

"The *right* Stone brother?" Deanna interrupted. Her mother's choice of words rubbed her the wrong way and put her defenses up. "What do you mean by that?"

Gayle took an infuriatingly long sip of her white wine before she answered. "It was terrible to see her with that snowboarder."

"Marcus?"

"Yes, Marcus."

"Why was it terrible?" She couldn't help herself. Not that Deanna didn't totally agree with her mother that Kylie was better suited to be with Malcolm, and that it was great to see her settled down and happy and all the rest of it, but to hear her mother speak about Marcus with such disdain definitely sparked something inside her. "What's wrong with Marcus?"

"What isn't wrong? Am I right, Jim?"

Deanna's father shrugged and turned his attention back to his beer.

"He was never faithful to her, for one thing," her mother continued. "And could you really expect he would be? He snowboards for a living. That's not a real job; it's an extended childhood and nothing but trouble can come from living that type of life. Traveling, surrounded by drugs and alcohol. I'm sure it's fine for some, but Marcus Stone is definitely not the type of man I'd want to see with any of you girls."

While her mother ranted about the evils of Marcus, Deanna went from feeling indignant to oddly smug, and by the time Samantha returned with their order of wings, a seed of an idea had been planted in Deanna's mind.

Chapter Three

A FEW MONTHS AGO, if someone had told Marcus he'd be standing on a ski hill owned by his brother, filling a snow pool with water in preparation for something called the Slush Cup, he would have laughed in their face and gone back to ripping down the hill on his board. But a lot had changed in a short time and the longer he spent in Cedar Springs, the further away his professional snowboarding career seemed.

"How's the pool coming?" Seth McBride, the manager of Stone Summit, and technically Marcus's boss, joined him at the end of the snow pool.

"This is the craziest thing I've ever seen." Marcus laughed. "I don't know how you got such an idea, or how you plan on convincing people to ski into a pool of ice water, but I don't think anyone will forget it anytime soon."

"That's the idea, right?" Seth had come up with the idea to close out the first ski season at Stone Summit with an absolutely wild idea of the Slush Cup, which basically involved people skiing down a run, off a small jump and into the slushy pool of water that Seth and Marcus were currently filling. There would be live music, barbecues, beer gardens, and prizes. Marcus had to admit, ever since he'd heard the idea, he'd been intrigued. It was just crazy enough to work and it certainly promised to be a good time.

"Is everything else in place? What do you need me to do, boss?" With the event, and closing weekend, only a few days away, it was definitely crunch time, but Marcus had to admit, even though Seth had been preoccupied with Cynthia and the news of their baby, he was completely dedicated to the event and pulling it off. "The Jacked Crackers are confirmed," Seth said. "We just need to finalize the stage preparations." They left the pool filling and walked as they talked. "You can oversee the stage?"

Marcus nodded. "I got it. And I'll get the beer garden fencing put up, too."

"Sounds good." Seth pulled out his phone and tapped some notes into it. "I just need to finalize some details about the barbecue and the beer gardens that Sam and Archer are going to coordinate, and we should be all set. Trent emailed me this morning to let me know the Spring's skiing packages have been completely sold out. It's going to be packed."

"And so much fun."

"Especially since you're going to kick off the event."

Marcus stopped in his tracks and stared at his friend. "What?"

"You heard me."

"No. I must have heard you wrong because what I thought you just said was that I was going to kick off the event." He crossed his arms and stared at Seth.

"That's right."

"Hell no. If you think I'm going to go flying into a pool of icy water, you have another think coming."

Seth tucked his phone away and turned to Marcus. "Come on. It'll be good press. Pro snowboarder Marcus Stone kicks off Slush Cup festivities." He held up his hands to indicate a headline but Marcus wasn't having any of it.

"No way."

"Think about it. It'll be good for your career, too."

Seth's words hit him like a blow. *Good for his career? What career?* He'd received an email the night before from his coach asking him whether he'd taken the test yet. They wanted to make sure he was back on the circuit for the next year and he'd mentioned something about a new movie to be filmed in the Swiss Alps in about a month's time that they wanted him for. If he was clean. Which of course he was. He always had been. The very thought of sullying his reputation by even taking another drug test pissed him off. He was a lot of things, but a drug user was not one of them. All he had to do was go to the doctor and take a drug test. Simple. Yet, all morning he'd picked up his phone and put it away again before he actually made the call to take the test.

"I told you I was off the circuit."

"Yeah, but..." Seth grinned. "Are you really? I mean, coming back to small-town life after what you've lived. Seriously?"

A few weeks ago, Marcus would have insisted that yes, he was ready to move back to town and settle into a normal albeit somewhat boring existence. Maybe he could even start looking seriously at designing snowboards, something he'd been dabbling with for the last few years. But that was before Deanna Gordon had shown up. The woman messed with his head and not in a good way. She was like a goddamned magnet that pulled him to her while at the same time repelled him. He thought he was over her. No, he *was* over her. He'd only felt love like that once. And once was enough, if it ended in the soul-crushing hurt it had caused. Nothing good had come from being with Deanna. Maybe it was time to get the hell out of town.

And maybe Seth had a point. An *appearance* at the Slush Cup might be good press and just what he needed to not only get back in his coach's good graces, but to really launch him to the top of his game and get him out of Cedar Springs again. At least for a while.

"I'll think about it."

That's all Seth needed to hear. He slapped Marcus on the back and smiled. "I knew it. Not that I want you to leave again, buddy. I'm getting kind of used to having you around again. But I knew there was something driving you to get back out there."

Marcus nodded along and tried to smile. Little did Seth know that the only thing that might drive him out of town again was the very same thing that made him want to stay. And all the conflict and chaos was due to one, very sexy, very crazy-making brunette. He pulled out his cell phone again. It was time to make that call after all. That way he'd have options and something told him, he'd need them.

BETWEEN PATIENTS, Deanna checked her email again. Still nothing. It had been almost a month since she'd placed the ads in the medical journals. Surely someone would want to move to Cedar Springs and take over a thriving practice.

A thriving practice full of sniffly noses, broken arms, and the occasional referral to a specialty clinic in nearby Calgary, which was the closest major center equipped to handle anything serious. Deanna missed the excitement of a big city ER with the car accidents, drug overdoses, and occasional bullet or knife wounds. But that was probably the appeal of living in a small town: those things were a whole lot less likely to happen.

There was no point dwelling on the current situation. It

was what it was and it wasn't all bad. It really was good to see her old friends again. She'd missed them. *And Marcus.*

No. Not Marcus.

She shut down that particular line of thought before it could take hold. Marcus and his sexy smile, knowing eyes, and oh good God his rock hard chest that had only gotten harder in the last few years, were not one of the positives of being in Cedar Springs. Quite the opposite, in fact.

But why?

That annoying little voice that she couldn't seem to shut up questioned her. And it was a good question. Years ago, her reasons for wanting to get away from Marcus Stone were completely different than any of the feelings she could possibly have for him now. Very different. He'd sparked something in her. Something that scared the hell out of her. Never in her whole life had she ever felt the way Marcus made her feel. It scared her senseless because he represented everything she'd been working hard to avoid: small town, settling down before she'd lived her life, getting stuck in the same town she'd grown up in. If she'd let herself love Marcus the way she'd wanted to, everything would have been different.

Different from what?

Another good, and totally infuriating, question from her subconscious. How had things turned out so differently than she'd dreamed of? Here she was, back in Cedar Springs, stuck for the foreseeable future, in the same place where she'd grown up. The only thing that was different was that she wasn't with Marcus.

Deanna dropped her pen on the pile of papers. "Dammit." Why did her subconscious have to be right? But it wasn't. Not totally, anyway. That wasn't the only thing that was different. She was a doctor now. And she might not be with Marcus, but she'd never really been with Marcus. That was part of the problem. He'd been with Kylie. All those years ago, despite what he'd said about love, she knew deep down she couldn't have been anything but one of the flings he was notorious for. Hell, Marcus wasn't the type of guy who did serious relationships. That was evidenced by the terrible and very public way he treated his girlfriend by always cheating on her. If she'd given everything up to be with him, he only would have broken her heart. Besides, Marcus Stone was not the kind of man she wanted to be with then, and it certainly wasn't the kind she wanted to be with now.

Nor was he the kind her parents wanted her to be with. Deanna almost laughed as she remembered the conversation from the night before at the Grizzly Paw. If her mother only knew about her history with Marcus, she'd freak. And she'd almost certainly change her tune about having Deanna stay in Cedar Springs to settle down.

Before she could let that thought percolate long, her phone buzzed with a message from Karen at the front desk. "Your next patient is here, Dr. Gordon. Room three."

Deanna pushed the button on her phone. "Thanks, Karen."

No time to think about what could have been; she actually had work to do. She straightened her jacket, hung her stethoscope around her neck and left her office for room three.

The patient's chart was in the slot outside of the door. Her dad refused to upgrade to an electronic system where the charts would all be sent via computers. If it were her practice —*whoa*. Better to shut that thought down right from the get-go, before it could take root. She was *not* staying. That was final.

She flipped through the chart and her initial reaction was to smile. Followed by a frown when she saw the reason for the visit.

Deanna rapped on the door before she turned the handle. "Hello."

Samantha Burke, or Harrison as Deanna continually had

trouble remembering, sat on the examination table and wore a paper gown. "Hi, Dee. Or should I call you Dr. Gordon? I'm sorry, I'm—"

"It's fine." Deanna smiled as warmly as she could in an effort to put her old friend at ease. Judging by the way her knee bounced up and down, she was clearly nervous to be at the doctor's office. Hopefully it wasn't just the fact that she was seeing Deanna that made her nervous. "I hope it's okay that you're seeing me today, Sam. Karen is supposed to clear it with people, but I know some slip through."

"I requested you, actually."

That surprised Deanna. "You did?"

Sam nodded. "I've been meaning to make an appointment with your dad for a while, but you know...it's one thing after another and pretty soon you forget. Besides, sometimes it's a little weird talking to a guy who's almost like an uncle about certain things, you know?"

Deanna laughed and settled onto her stool. "I do. Trust me." She flipped open the chart and smiled. "It says here that you're thinking about starting a family. That's exciting."

But the look on Samantha's face was anything but excited.

"Is that your idea?" Deanna continued. "Or Trent's? Because if you're not ready to be a mother yet, I'm sure that—"

"It's not that."

Deanna waited. She'd had plenty of experience with patients who needed a little time to divulge the real reason for their visit and it seemed as if Samantha would be one of those patients. "Why don't you tell me what's going on?"

"Well..." Sam looked down at her lap. The move was so unlike the strong, self-assured Samantha Deanna knew from the past, that it took her a bit off guard, but Deanna bided her time. "With Carmen and Dylan having little Hunter, it kind of got us thinking, you know?" Deanna nodded. "So we thought we'd start trying."

"Trying's the fun part."

That made Sam smile. "It really is. But...it's not working."

And there it was. The real reason for her visit. Conception issues were more common than most people realized. But most of the time it was fairly straightforward. "Okay. Not to worry. It's early and you're young and we'll figure it out, okay? Let's start with a few questions."

Deanna ran through her usual questions about the patient's health, sex life, and menstrual cycle. When she was finished with the questioning, she conducted a simple exam.

"Okay," Deanna said as she finished up. "Why don't you get dressed and join me in my office so we can talk about a few options?"

"It won't take too long, will it?" Sam sat up and adjusted her paper gown. "Because I have to get back to the Paw. Archer wanted to talk to me about something and I know he's going to insist that I hire some more help, but—"

"It won't take long." Deanna smiled and added another note to her chart. Samantha's work stress was definitely a factor that shouldn't be overlooked, but something told her she might not want to mention it at that exact moment. "I'll meet you there in a minute."

It was almost literally only a minute before Sam knocked on her door and let herself into Deanna's office. She perched on the chair across from the desk and immediately fidgeted with her cell phone. "So what do you think, Doc?"

Deanna laughed and shook her head. She'd never get used to her old friends calling her Doctor. "I think you're fine." Deanna got right to the point. "I think you're young and healthy and there isn't any reason to be concerned at this point."

"But we're not pregnant yet."

"No." Deanna tried not to smile. "But you said yourself you only stopped taking the Pill a few months ago, and sometimes it takes the body a few months to work everything out. My advice is to keep trying and keep having fun. Because really, trying is the fun part and from what I understand, once the baby does come, there's a whole lot less time for that."

Sam nodded reluctantly and it was easy to see that Deanna hadn't given her the news that she'd been looking for. Not that she thought her old friend was looking for a bad diagnosis, but she'd seen this type of reaction before with busy professionals. When it came to their health, they wanted quick answers that could be solved with a pill or precise formula. "So there's nothing I can take that will help things along?"

"There's no fertility pill that will magically knock you up, if that's what you're asking. If you really want my advice, Sam, I'd tell you to slow down, relax a little and have fun. When you're stressed, your body is a less hospitable environment for conception. Honestly, there really isn't a reason to panic. If you guys have been trying for twelve months and still there's nothing, then we can look at some other alternatives."

"A year?"

"I know it seems like a long time, but it's really not." Deanna stood to indicate the appointment was over. "Trust me, okay?"

Samantha nodded and stood. "Everyone is telling me the same thing."

"To slow down?" Sam nodded. "It's good advice."

"Maybe so." Samantha seemed to be lost in her own thoughts for a second before her bright smile returned. "Well, I guess I should get going and go talk to Archer. He probably has some sort of new menu ideas or something."

"And maybe you'll talk about hiring someone?" Deanna walked to the door and turned the handle.

"I will."

She watched Sam walk down the hallway and returned to her desk just in time for the phone to buzz. Karen's voice came over the speaker. "Your next patient is waiting in room two. I told him you were running a little late, but he's a bit agitated."

Crap.

Deanna hated being one of those doctors who ran late and she tried hard to keep to her schedule, but if it meant spending a few extra minutes with her patients to build a relationship, then she would. She refused to sacrifice quality care just for the sake of going a few minutes over time.

"Thanks, Karen. I'm on it."

She took a quick sip from her water bottle and headed out to see her next patient.

―――――

IT WAS bad enough he had to spend his afternoon in town in the doctor's office when he should have been up at Stone Summit, but when the doctor was running late? That just made it worse. There were a million things to do, and Marcus hated visiting the doctor on a good day, let alone when he had to deal with such an annoying situation. Not only was it embarrassing to go in for a drug test, he had a feeling that Dr. Gordon wasn't going to make it easy on him. Hell, the man already thought Marcus was the *bad* twin and his brother walked on water, but he was also Deanna's father. A fact that only made the whole situation even more uncomfortable. Even if Dr. Gordon had no idea of his history with Deanna. Marcus did, and that was enough.

He'd thought about going into the city to deal with the drug test, but it was better to just get it over with. When he'd phoned and the receptionist fit him in for an afternoon appointment, it just seemed easier to deal with whatever judgment the old man passed down.

"If he ever shows up," Marcus muttered and paced the small room for the hundredth time. "What is it with doctors anyway?" That could have meant a million things, especially considering the only doctor he had any real opinion on these days was Deanna. Thankfully he didn't have time to think about it because there was a knock on the door. "It's about time," he said under his breath as the door swung open.

The second the door opened, Marcus wanted it to close again because there had to be some sort of mistake. "What are you doing here?"

Deanna stood there, looking way too sexy in her white coat with her thick, black hair pulled back into some kind of knot on the back of her head. She held a file in her hands and stared at him with a cold, professional detachment that made Marcus want to tug the knot out of her hair and kiss her senseless until there was some warmth back on that beautiful face.

"You have an appointment."

"No," he said. "I have an appointment with Dr. Gordon."

"I am Dr. Gordon," she said unnecessarily.

"I know you're Dr. Gordon. But you are not the Dr. Gordon I came to see."

She dropped the file onto the examination bed and crossed her arms. "Then you'll have to reschedule because I'm the only doctor on today and from what I understand, you sweet-talked the receptionist to get this appointment, so there must be a damned good reason."

Dammit. Maybe he had used a little charm to get the appointment, but the last thing he needed was Deanna thinking he'd done it so he could see her. Quite the opposite, really.

"That's not how it was at all," he said. "Whatever you're thinking...it's wrong."

"What I'm thinking is that I have a very full schedule today, so if you think making an unnecessary appointment with me is in anyway going to soften me up for—"

"For what?"

Her face turned a sexy shade of red, but her eyes were hard when she crossed her arms over her chest. "Look, do you need to see a doctor or not?"

Marcus was running out of choices. He really didn't want to disclose the truth to Deanna, but wasn't she the entire reason he was taking the test anyway? When it came to Deanna, he was going to need options. And living in close proximity seemed less and less like a viable one. If she was going to stay in Cedar Springs, he wasn't. Period. Which meant...

"Yes," he relented after a moment. "I do need an appointment. But I need your word that it will remain confidential."

Something flickered over her face. "Why wouldn't it?"

"I know you have a doctor's code or whatever," he said. "But I also know it's a small town and I really need this to stay between us. No one can find out. Especially Malcolm."

That was the other problem with taking a drug test in a small town. If word got back to Malcolm, he'd not only be livid, he might fire him. And word would no doubt get back to his sponsors and they'd drop him before the results were even back. It was one thing to quietly be suspended from the circuit, but if the media found out the reason, innocent or not, Marcus's career would be over.

Deanna nodded and waved her hand to dismiss his concerns. "Whatever. Of course." She picked up the chart and sat on her little stool before she flipped it open. "So what can I do for you today?"

Marcus swallowed hard. "I need a drug test."

The words hung in the small room and if it wasn't for the tense way she held her body, he might have thought she hadn't heard him. She had. There was no doubt.

"You need a what?"

"I don't do drugs."

"But you need a test?"

"Yes. To prove I'm clean."

"So you did them in the past?"

"What? No." He scrubbed a hand over his face. "Look, it's a long story, but I need a test to prove I'm clean so I can get back on the professional circuit. Can you do it?"

He was beginning to question her professionalism and his own poor choice for not going to the city to get the test, when she finally spoke.

"Yes," she said slowly. "I can do it."

"And you'll keep it quiet?"

A wicked little smile slid over her gorgeous face and she tapped her pen on the file before she pointed it at him. "That all depends," she said. "I think we can work something out."

WORK SOMETHING OUT? Had she really just said that? What was wrong with her?

Deanna knew exactly what was wrong with her and he stood dangerously close to her. From the moment she'd picked up his file outside the door and saw Marcus's name written there, her heart had beat out of control and she'd had to work hard to control her breathing so he wouldn't see the effect he still had on her.

"What do you mean?" he asked.

It was a good question and one that Deanna didn't really have a fully formed answer for. The truth was, the idea had flown into her head so fast she didn't have time to think it through all the way. And now that the words were out there, she couldn't back down. There was no way she could say something like *never mind* or *it's nothing* after that. Not without looking like a total idiot and where Marcus was involved, she seemed to do a pretty good job of that anyway. But to say what she was thinking...it went against every ethical code she'd sworn to and she was not that type of person. She was running out of choices, and maybe doing one bad—okay, not even bad, but slightly wrong—thing was justified now and then? She took a deep breath and made her decision.

"What I mean is, if you want me to stay quiet, I'll need you to do me a favor in return." She clenched the pen in her hand so tightly she was surprised it didn't break. But she needed to stay in control. She couldn't let him see that she was nervous or unsure. She needed the upper hand.

"Are you kidding me?"

"Not at all."

"Isn't it your job to give me the test?"

"Yes."

"And isn't it part of your code of conduct or something to remain quiet about it?"

Dammit. He wasn't going to make this easy. "Technically," she said slowly. His self-satisfied grin made her want to slap him, but she forced herself to stay calm. "But like you said, it's a small town and things have a way of slipping out. I cannot control what happens with the nurses or the lab technicians, and never mind what—"

"Fine." The grin was gone. His face was a hard mask of stone, which caused a twitch of guilt in her gut. "What do you want?"

"I want you to date me."

The words hung in the air and immediately after she'd spoken them aloud, Deanna wanted to pull them back and rephrase it to make her look less desperate. A whole lot less desperate, because no matter how it sounded, that was not what she intended.

"You want to date?"

"No. Well, yes. But not really."

"I'm confused." He shook his head.

She took a deep breath and straightened her shoulders before she tried to explain her half-cocked idea that she'd only just come up with. "Look, it's no secret that I don't want to stay in Cedar Springs, but my parents are pushing really hard for me to settle down here and meet a nice guy."

Marcus tilted his head and raised an eyebrow. "So you think I'm that nice guy?"

"Quite the opposite, really. My dad really doesn't like you and they both think you're exactly the wrong type of guy for me, so if they think I'm serious with you, they'll be much more likely to support my move back to Toronto." As she spoke her idea out loud for the first time, she couldn't decide whether it really was genius or ridiculous. Either way, it was the only plan she had and she could use any advantage that she could get. Besides, now that she'd voiced it, she couldn't take it back. She had to commit.

"Okay, wait." Marcus ran a hand through his hair so it flopped over one eye in a way that sent a flare of desire through her. "Let me get this straight. You're blackmailing me to fake date you because your parents don't like me in exchange for doing your job the way you should be doing it anyway?"

Well, dammit, when he put it like that, it didn't sound good at all. She wasn't being unethical. Okay, well, she wasn't *trying* to be unethical. She was just trying to help them both. At least that's what she was going to tell herself. "It's not blackmail."

He stared at her hard. "What would you call it?"

HE DIDN'T TAKE his gaze off her, mostly because he knew it was making her nervous, but also because she was so damn sexy and despite the crazy things coming out of her mouth, and all the pent-up anger he had for her for leaving him hanging all those years ago, his body reacted hard and fast just by being close to her. It had always been that way between them. A chemistry that went beyond the physical, and that was part of the problem. No, that was the *whole* problem. And now she was suggesting some ridiculous blackmail plan? There was no way. Never mind the fact that she was being unethical and borderline illegal; he couldn't survive it. The woman made him feel things he'd never felt—hell, that he had no business feeling. And she made him want things he'd never wanted before. Even after rejecting him, he still wanted her and he'd be dammed if he'd be played again. There was no way he was going to voluntarily spend more time with her. That was the whole reason for getting the damned drug test. The more distance he could put between them, the better. Except...he let his imagination drift to what spending more time with Deanna might actually mean.

Deanna pushed up from the stool and straightened her white coat. "Look, I'm going to be honest with you, okay?"

"That would be refreshing."

She gave him a look, but he ignored it and waited for her to continue.

"I know it's not an ideal situation."

"No, it's not."

Even as he spoke the words, his mind went wild with potential scenarios he could picture himself in with Deanna as his *fake girlfriend*. It might not be ideal, but if his imagination was anything to go on, there might be some benefits. Such as having her in his bed again. And damn, that was certainly a benefit.

She glared at him and he gestured for her to continue. "And I'm not really trying to bribe you."

"Yes you are."

"Okay, I am," she admitted. "I know it's not really my style."

"No." He shook his head. "It's not your style." He crossed his arms and gave her a grin. "But people change." He knew he was being an asshole, but he couldn't help it. He clearly had her in a tight spot. Or was it her who had him in a tight spot? The entire conversation had taken him so completely off guard, he no longer knew what the hell was going on. But now that he had an image of her naked and underneath him, he couldn't shake it.

"The way I see it, it's a win-win scenario for both of us." She tucked her pen into the knot in her hair and crossed her arms; her breasts pressed up tight against her white coat, so Marcus had to look away. "You get what you need and I get enough ammunition to convince my parents I should get out of here."

"Why don't you just tell them what you want? You're not a child anymore."

"It's not that easy."

It seemed easy enough to Marcus, but from what he remembered about Deanna's family dynamics, they were a whole lot different than what he was used to. "That's right," he said with a smug grin. "You always did do whatever Mommy and Daddy wanted." He knew he was being an ass, but he couldn't stop himself. Besides, he wasn't a fool. He knew her parents' approval, or what would be the lack thereof, had a whole lot to do with the reason Deanna had run away from him all those years ago.

"That's not fair."

He only raised his eyebrow in response and used the opportunity to run through the pros and cons of her ridiculous proposal. He didn't owe her a damn thing. No, what he owed her was a dose of what she'd dealt to him: a broken heart, wounded pride and...a grin crept across his face. Maybe that was exactly what he owed her. And maybe that's exactly what he'd give her.

Marcus had enough experience with women to know when one was attracted to him, and it was easy to see by the blush on her face, and the way she couldn't quite catch her breath—never mind the way she'd been flirting with him on the hill the other day—Deanna was still attracted to him. Even if she didn't know it. It probably wouldn't take much effort to convince her that she still had feelings for him, especially if they were pretending to be a couple. And when she fell for him again, and looked into his eyes to tell him that she'd been wrong and she still loved him, that's when Marcus would make sure she knew exactly how it felt to have your heart broken.

The idea took shape in his mind and he brushed back the kernel of guilt that came with it. Before he could change his mind, he nodded. "You have a deal. But I have a few rules."

Chapter Four

THE SPRING SUN WARMED HER, and Deanna probably didn't even need a jacket as she walked down Main Street toward Dream Puffs, where she'd promised to meet Cynthia for a cup of tea. But despite the warmth of the day, she couldn't seem to shake the chill she'd felt ever since she'd sat in her examination room with Marcus and listened to his *rules* for the stupid deal she'd come up with. From the moment they shook on it, and a shot of desire had raced all the way through her at his touch, she knew she'd made a deal with the devil.

Of course, the whole plan had come to her so quickly it's not as though she'd really had time to work out the finer points in her head, but she hadn't even thought of some of the things Marcus had made her agree to. His rules were actually quite simple, and they made sense if she was going to pull off her deception, but it irked her to give him any credit at all. His first rule was that they couldn't tell anyone the truth. That meant she had to lie to her friends, too. Not just her parents. Deanna wasn't a liar by nature. The only other time she could remember keeping such a secret also had to do with Marcus, and that time had almost killed her. But she could see the logic.

It was a small town, and they couldn't risk the truth getting back to her parents. As much as she hated to agree to it, she did.

The second rule was much simpler and easy to agree to. Especially because it would only cement what they were trying to do. Marcus insisted that they be seen in public together. That was an easy one for her to agree to. It would make their story more believable. She had no objections.

And then they shook on it and just like that, the deal was made. She should feel some sort of sense of relief. It probably wouldn't take long at all for her parents to find out and lose their minds about her new boyfriend. She had to stay strong and there was no doubt her dad would get on board with the associate hunt in no time.

Until then, she just had to make the story believable. Starting with her friends. Deanna took a deep breath, straightened her long hair over her shoulder and pushed open the door to the bakery. At once she was greeted by the familiar aroma of cinnamon and fresh baking. She inhaled deeply and savored it because that's as close as she would get to enjoying the decadent treats. Those delicious cinnamon buns would go straight to her hips and she had enough curves already. She definitely didn't need any padding.

But Marcus always liked your curves. The thought came out of nowhere and took her off guard. It didn't matter that Marcus used to run his hands down her body, lingering at the dip in her waist and the swell of her hips. The point was moot. He wouldn't be doing it again.

"Dee!"

She managed to shake herself out of her thoughts long enough to focus across the room to where Cynthia sat. But she wasn't alone. Kylie sat next to her and waved in Deanna's direction with a warm smile on her face.

Crap. It was a struggle, but Deanna managed not to let her smile falter.

She hadn't expected Kylie to be there. It was going to make her telling her friends about her new *relationship* a bit trickier. Possibly quite a bit. Deanna forced her feet to move across the cafe until she stood at the table.

"Kylie," she said. "What a surprise. I thought you would have been back in Vancouver by now at school."

"Oh no. Malcolm's convinced me to stay for the Slush Cup tomorrow." She laughed, looking happier than Deanna ever remembered. "Apparently it's quite a big deal."

"Seth is certainly excited about it," Cynthia added. "Dee, sit down. We ordered you a tea latte and a cinnamon bun. I hope that's okay?"

She nodded dumbly and slid into the chair across from them. "That's great. Thank you." Maybe a little comfort food wouldn't hurt after all. She might need the sustenance to get her through what she was about to say.

"It's so good to see you," Cynthia said. "It's been way too long. I just don't understand how you could be gone from home so long."

"Oh, come on, Cyn." Kylie smiled warmly. "Deanna has always had her sights set on bigger and better things. But it is good to see you. I know your parents want you to stay. But what are your plans, really? It would be so cool if we could work together once I have my nursing license. Can you imagine?"

Deanna couldn't imagine. But mostly because Kylie would probably never want to talk to her again after she found out about what Deanna had done with Marcus all those years ago. She'd been a shitty friend. Of that there was no doubt. She took a sip of her latte to keep from answering Kylie.

"So tell me about the baby." It would definitely be easier to shift the conversation to Cynthia for a while and it worked.

Cynthia filled the next fifteen minutes talking about her upcoming pregnancy and how they planned to name the child after her recently departed mother. They exchanged hugs and Deanna passed on her condolences, but then the conversation shifted again.

"Enough about me." Cynthia wiped her eyes. "You didn't answer the question."

"What question was that?" Deanna looked between the two women.

"What are your plans? Are you really going to go back to Toronto or are you going to settle in here for a while?"

It was the perfect time to tell them about her and Marcus. Or at least, her story about the two of them. She'd rehearsed what she was going to say before she'd arrived, but that was when it was only Cynthia who would hear the news. Deanna had figured Cynthia might be a little happy about the fact that she was dating someone. Even if it was Marcus. But Kylie? She had no idea how Kylie would react and that was without knowing the whole truth. Because there was no way in hell she was telling her that. At least not now.

"Well," she started. "I actually have—"

Her cell phone buzzed and cut her off.

"Excuse me." She reached for her phone. "Just in case it's the clinic."

"Of course." Kylie smiled.

It wasn't the clinic.

Did you tell her?

Marcus. She'd made the mistake of telling him that she had plans to meet Cynthia and of course he thought it was the perfect opportunity to start sowing the seeds of their arrangement. Logically she knew that if they were going to go through with the plan, she was going to have to say something sooner or later, but now that it was time to do it, she was definitely getting cold feet.

No, she tapped back. The response came immediately.

It was your idea. If you don't go through with it, deal is off.

Dammit.

I can't, she typed back and looked up long enough to smile apologetically at her friends. "It'll just be a minute." *Kylie's here, too.*

Marcus's response took a beat longer, but when it came, Deanna had to struggle to keep her face neutral. *Doesn't change anything.* He knew damn well it changed things.

Marcus, I— Before she could finish typing, her response was cut off with a new text.

Seth is here. I'm going to hold up my end. Better tell them. Cynthia's phone will ring soon.

Damn. If Marcus told Seth, there was no doubt that he'd be on the phone with his girlfriend in seconds to relay the information. If Deanna didn't tell her first, it would look bad. Very bad. She shoved her phone back in her purse and looked up at the girls.

"Sorry about that." She smiled and pulled a piece of pastry off the bun. "Where were we?" She shoved it in her mouth.

"You were going to tell us your plans." Kylie nodded to her purse. "Is everything okay?"

"Oh yeah." Deanna waved away her question. "Just a little confusion over a lab result." *Wow, the lying thing was getting easier and easier.* Might as well jump in all the way. "So there was actually something I was going to tell you." The women leaned forward eagerly and Deanna forced her smile even wider. "I'm actually seeing someone. It's been kind of—"

"Who?"

She turned to Cynthia, who of course got right to the point. Deanna made eye contact with her, carefully avoiding Kylie when she said, "Marcus Stone."

"What?" Cynthia's mouth fell open. "Marcus? How? When? Why?"

She ignored Cynthia's questions and turned to look at Kylie, who hadn't said anything. Her old friend watched her carefully, but still hadn't spoken. "Kylie? I hope it's not strange or anything. I know you guys have history. It just kind of happened and—"

"How?" Cynthia asked the question again. "I mean, you've only just gotten back."

"Well, I've been back for a few weeks now." Deanna launched into her carefully rehearsed story. "And I guess when we were out snowboarding the other day, we just kind of connected. There was an attraction there."

"Wow." Cynthia's face split into a broad smile. "Well, that's great. Right, Kylie?"

All eyes turned to Kylie, who still looked at Deanna suspiciously. "Yes," she finally said. "It's great."

"It's not weird?" Deanna knew it was weird. Hell, it was more than just a little weird. But Kylie didn't know the half of it. "I mean, it's okay?"

Kylie nodded and finally smiled. "Of course it's fine. Why wouldn't it be? Marcus and I are ancient history. Besides, I'm engaged to be married and I've never been happier."

They all toasted with their lattes and soon the conversation drifted into other topics. When she snuck off the bathroom, Deanna pulled out her phone and texted Marcus.

I told them.

The response came at once. *Good. See you tomorrow, lover.*

Her face burned and she shoved the phone into her purse. He'd tricked her into telling them. Not that she'd had any other choice. But still. Marcus didn't need to think he was in control. It was bad enough he was being a first-class asshole. She'd more or less expected him to be a jerk after the way she'd stood him up and, after all, it was *she* who was blackmailing *him*. But it didn't make it sting any less.

"WHAT'S SO IMPORTANT?"

Marcus snapped his head up from his phone that he'd stared at ever since he'd sent that last text. The second he'd hit Send, he'd regretted it. He'd sounded like a total ass and even if he felt like one for what he planned to do to Deanna, it wasn't going to help anything if he actually behaved like one. Judging from the lack of response from her, no doubt she thought he was an ass, too.

"It's nothing." Marcus jammed his phone in his back pocket. "Where are we at with everything?"

The men, along with Malcolm and every other free staff member at Stone Summit, had been busy all day putting the finishing touches on the hill for the Slush Cup. And it looked great. The slush pool at the base was completely ready and being guarded to ensure no one decided to do a test run. The stage was set up, the beer gardens were ready, and the registration desk had been fielding requests all day to enter the competition. Marcus had definitely been skeptical when Seth had come up with the idea. No way were people going to pay money to ski off a jump and land in a giant pool of icy-cold water.

But they were. And not only that, they were excited about it.

The buzz around the hill grew into a frenzy. Everyone was excited about the events and Seth was right, there was going to be costumes. But not for him. It was bad enough Seth had roped him into actually participating. There was no way he was going to dress up in some stupid costume.

"So did you choose your costume, brother?" It was as if Malcolm could read his mind. His brother slapped him on the back and then quickly dodged the punch Marcus halfheartedly threw in his direction.

"No way." He turned back to the snow fence he was fastening into place. "I agreed to do the stupid jump. I'm not dressing up."

"Oh, come on. You'll disappoint all your fans."

Marcus raised an eyebrow. "Does anyone even know I'm doing it?" When the other two men exchanged looks, Marcus got a sinking feeling. "You didn't...."

"We only called a few reporters," Seth said. "And the major news stations in Calgary." Marcus felt his temper rise but he couldn't get too mad, not really. He'd known it was going to happen.

"Oh, and don't forget the reporter from *Shred*," Malcolm added.

"*Shred?*"

"Oh, right. I don't know how I could've forgotten about her."

Marcus glared at Seth, who grinned. He hadn't forgotten about a damn thing. "*Shred?* You have the biggest snowboarding publication coming to cover the event?"

Seth nodded smugly and rightly so; it was a big coup. "I told you it would be good for your career. The reporter, April Easton, was excited to hear you were going back to the circuit."

"Well, I didn't really say I was going to—"

"And she thought the Slush Cup would be a great way to announce your return."

"Of course she did," Marcus mumbled.

Malcolm grabbed the end of the snow fence and tugged. "So it better be good, Marc. You're going to need a costume."

"Right." He abandoned the fence and grabbed his gloves out of his pocket.

The guys worked for a few more minutes in silence before Malcolm started to talk about Kylie and how he'd convinced her to stay through the weekend, which reminded Marcus of the fact that Deanna had just told Cynthia and Kylie their story. And whether he'd changed his mind or not, the deception was in play. Not that he had changed his mind. In fact, the more he thought about it the night before, the more resolute he was that he could pull it off. By the time they were done playing their little game, he was determined to show Deanna exactly how badly it could hurt to have your heart broken. And he didn't feel a damned bit bad about it. Well, not really. But whatever feelings of doubt he had, he just had to keep shoving them down. There was no room for real feelings when it came to a situation like this one.

"So the girls are going to be up here all day tomorrow?"

Seth and Malcolm looked at him as if he'd lost his mind. "Of course. The whole town is going to be here," Seth said. "You do know that, right?"

He nodded, because he did know. But until that moment, Marcus hadn't really thought about what that meant. The whole town would be there and they'd all see Marcus and Deanna together.

"So I'm going to be bringing a date, too."

Just as he knew they would, the guys laughed. "Right. Which one of your ski bunnies are you—"

"Seriously," Marcus cut Malcolm off. "I'm dating someone." He waited, because he knew the inevitable questions would start. Just as soon as they recovered from the shock. The recovery happened faster than Marcus expected and they both fired questions at him.

"When?"

"What's her name?"

"Is she real?"

"Do we know her?"

Marcus laughed. "Yes she's real," he answered first. "And yes, you know her. Actually, we've known each other for years and we just reconnected the other day on the slopes. Her name is Deanna Gordon." He held his breath after that final detail and waited for the fallout. And he knew there would be one.

Seth recovered from the shock first. Instead of another question, he laughed.

"What's so funny?" Marcus looked from Seth to Malcolm and back. "Seriously?"

"Deanna Gordon?" Seth managed between chuckles. "You?"

"That's hard to believe?" Marcus looked to his brother and ignored Seth. "Is it?"

Malcolm shrugged. "A little."

Marcus had expected a reaction from the guys, maybe one of bewilderment that he'd settled down or was being serious with a girl—he'd even expected them to be impressed that he had hooked up with the good doctor—but he hadn't expected them to find it funny or hard to believe. He curled his fists next to his sides and gritted his teeth. "Why is that?"

Seth somehow managed to swallow his laughter enough to say, "Because she's Deanna and you are..."

"You," Malcolm finished for him. "Don't take this the wrong way, Marcus, but you're kind of a...free spirit and maybe even a little..."

"Immature."

"Immature?" Marcus glared at Seth. "I am not immature."

"Okay," Malcolm intervened. "It's not that you're immature so much as you're not really the relationship type."

"And he is?" Marcus pointed at Seth, who up until a few months ago was known for his playboy ways. At least until he'd fallen in love with Cynthia.

"That's different."

"It's not."

"It's just that...Deanna?" Malcolm asked. "She's such a..."

Marcus's jaw twitched as he waited for him to finish that sentence. Twin brother or not, he wouldn't hesitate to throw a punch if Malcolm said one word against Deanna. "Such a what, brother?"

Malcolm held up his hands in defense. "Calm down, man. I was just going to say that she's such a good girl and you are definitely not. But if you're getting that worked up about it, you must really like her."

Malcolm's words took him off guard and Marcus took a step back. That's not why he was getting defensive of Deanna. Hell no. He'd get defensive about...anyone he was interested in. He shook his head, more to convince himself than anything else. It wasn't like that with Deanna. It was all for a purpose. Nothing more.

"Hey." Seth spoke up. "I'm all for it. If you're happy, we're happy, man." He slapped Marcus's back and Marcus turned to look at him. He hated lying to the guys, but there didn't seem to be a choice. At least not for now. It was a means to an end. That was all and that's what he was going to keep telling himself.

He nodded absently. "I'm happy."

"Good." Malcolm gave the snow fence a tug and gestured with his head. "Then go secure the far end. We need to get this fence up."

Marcus shook his head. "I'm sure Seth's got this." He grabbed his gloves out of his pocket and stuffed his hands in them as he took a step back. He needed to clear his head and refocus, and the best way he knew to do that was to go shred some powder on his board.

"Where the hell are you going?" Seth called out behind him as he walked away.

Marcus turned long enough to see Malcolm shake his head. But he was smiling and that was a good sign. "I thought I'd go check things out at the top of the Gold chair."

"Right." Malcolm winked. He knew enough to know when Marcus needed some time alone and although he was sure he'd hear about his vanishing act later, Marcus cared more about getting out on the hill alone to clear his head.

THE AIR at the top of the Gold chair, the highest chairlift they had at Stone Summit, was cool. It may be spring, but seasons had a very different meaning on a mountain. Marcus zipped his jacket and sat in the snow to buckle his boots into the bindings. Sitting at the top of the hill, looking out over the run he was about to experience, had always been his favorite part of snowboarding. There was so much potential in those few moments before everything started to happen.

He took a deep breath and exhaled slowly; the stress from earlier and all the mixed-up feelings surrounding Deanna and the fake relationship that hadn't even really started yet slipped away, at least for the moment. He was about to reach up and pull his goggles off his helmet when a voice stopped him.

"No way!"

He turned to his right and the direction of the voice. A kid —he couldn't have been much older than twelve or thirteen— sat less than a foot away from him, gawking with his mouth hanging open.

"You're Marcus Stone," the kid said. "You're, like, the *King of the Board*. My friends are never gonna believe this."

Marcus nodded and smiled. He'd grown fairly used to being recognized on ski hills. It went with the touristy stuff and unlike some of the other guys on the circuit, he enjoyed every second of it. Usually. He stuck out his hand. It would only take a minute to chat with the kid and then he could take his run.

"I am." They shook gloved hands. "What's your name?"

"Dresden. But I hate it. Call me Dre."

"Good to meet you, Dre. I like your board." He pointed to

the kid's snowboard that was so completely covered with stickers Marcus couldn't make out the brand.

"Nah." Dre flipped snow over his board. "It's so old and crappy. I wanted a new one for Christmas, but I got a PlayStation instead."

"A PlayStation? That sounds awesome."

"Not when all I want to do is be on the hill." Dre shrugged. "Besides, I have to share it with my sister."

Marcus laughed. The kid reminded him so much of himself at that age. All he wanted to do was be outside shredding powder. He lived for it and he probably would have been disappointed with a top-of-the-line video gaming system, too. "Well, it's not always about the board," he said. "It's about the guy *on* the board."

"Easy for you to say. Look at your ride."

It was true: Marcus had a top-of-the-line Burton board, compliments of his biggest sponsor. In fact, he had a half-dozen boards, all of them worth thousands. None of them were the board he really wanted to be riding. Those boards were in a sketchbook in his desk. He'd started work on a prototype, but that had been on hold ever since he'd been back in Cedar Springs.

"It's true," Marcus said. "I've been pretty lucky. But I mean it." He pointed to the kid. "The board is only part of it. Most of it comes from the guy strapped to the board."

"Whatever." Dre hung his head and picked at the snow.

Suddenly, Marcus's brain-clearing run down the slopes no longer seemed like a great idea.

"Come on," Marcus said. "I'll show you."

Dre's head popped up, his eyes huge. "What?"

"Come on." Marcus pushed himself up to standing. "Let's see what you got."

"Seriously? You're gonna ride with me?"

"It's the only way to see what you got." Marcus pulled his goggles down onto his face. "You coming?"

Dre scrambled up and confidently pushed off, heading down the hill. Marcus didn't even bother to hide his smile as he followed suit.

Chapter Five

DEANNA'S ALARM went off at seven. Typically it would have been far too early for a Saturday morning, but she'd already been up most of the night tossing and turning and mostly stressing about the upcoming day, so the alarm was actually a relief that she didn't need to bother pretending to sleep anymore.

She turned it off before she lay in her bed and stared at the ceiling for another few minutes to try to build her strength to face the day. It was the Slush Cup, which meant if she thought telling Kylie and Cynthia about her fake relationship with Marcus was hard, she was in for a very challenging day. From the way everyone was buzzing, the whole town would be up at Stone Summit for the festivities. Her deception was about to go public.

"No point putting it off," she said to the poster of Ashton Kutcher in his *That '70s Show* days. She was really going to have to update the room. Not that she planned to stay. But still, there was something inherently weird about a woman who was almost thirty sleeping in her high school bedroom.

Deanna groaned and rolled out of bed. The second she

opened her bedroom door, the mouth-watering aroma of bacon and pancakes hit her and her stomach growled. Her mother's cooking was amazing, but it wasn't doing much for her waistline. If she wasn't careful, her curves were going to get even curvier before she managed to get out of Cedar Springs.

"Deanna?" Her mother's voice called out before she could get across the hall to the bathroom. "Is that you?"

She rolled her eyes. *As if it would be anyone else creeping around the upstairs hallway.* "Yes, Mom."

"Your breakfast is ready."

"None for me, Mom. I'm just going to hop in the shower." She didn't wait for her mother's response before she closed the bathroom door, locking it behind her because it would definitely not be out of the realm of possibilities for her mother to bring her breakfast into the bathroom if it meant she'd eat a home-cooked, hearty breakfast.

Deanna took longer getting ready than she normally would; as a medical student and then busy resident, she'd mastered the quick shower, hair up, and a slick of mascara routine that got her through most days. But today was not an ordinary day, and not only was she trying to avoid her parents for a few extra minutes, she definitely required the armor of a perfectly put together appearance if she had to deal with Marcus Stone all day. And that's exactly what was on the agenda.

She blew out her long, dark hair before plaiting it in a thick braid that hung over her shoulder. She carefully applied eyeliner and just a swipe of shadow to make her eyes pop before she added a slick of lip gloss. The day would be primarily spent outside, so she dressed in leggings to wear under her snowboarding pants, with a tight red t-shirt under her sweater so she'd be prepared when the sun came out. Red was Marcus's favorite color, a detail she remembered vividly because it had involved a red lace bra and panty set and his strong, sure hands removing them.

When she had finished, she gave herself one last once-over in the mirror before she headed downstairs, where hopefully she could grab a quick cup of coffee and escape for the day.

No such luck. The second she walked into the kitchen, her father put down his paper and her mother jumped up from her chair. "Your breakfast is a little cold." She popped the plate in the microwave. "But I'll get it fixed right up for you."

"Mom, I'm good." Deanna poured herself a cup of coffee. "Just coffee for me this morning."

"Nonsense." The microwave beeped and Gayle put the plate in Deanna's spot at the table. "Now sit and eat. You're going up to the hill today, aren't you?"

Deanna nodded.

"Then you need your nourishment. Eat."

Dutifully, Deanna sat and used her fork to cut off a piece of pancake.

"You look nice." Her father smiled and took a sip of his coffee.

"Thanks." She chewed the pancake slowly and fiddled with her fork. Despite the fact that the whole idea of lying to her parents—and everyone else—had been her idea, it didn't make it any easier to sit across from them knowing that by the end of the day they were going to be disappointed in her, all because of her choice of boyfriend. Her whole life, Deanna had always done what would make her mom and dad happy. Purposely hurting them went against everything she'd ever known. But it was for a good cause. She swallowed the pancake that had turned to sawdust in her mouth and took a sip of coffee. She had to keep remembering that. *All of it was for a reason.* And she needed to stick to her plan.

"Is everything okay, dear? Is the pancake still cold?" Her mother watched her, worried.

"I'm good, Mom. Honestly. I'm just running a little late today. I wanted to stop in at the office and check on a few lab results before I went up to Stone Summit."

"See?" Her dad slapped the paper to the table. "You're the perfect doctor for this town. So conscientious. Your attention to detail is impeccable."

"Hardly, Dad." Deanna pushed the plate away and stood. "And it won't work. You're not going to convince me that Cedar Springs is where I need to be."

"Well, if you—"

"Dad."

He closed his mouth.

Deanna grabbed her coat and purse and was just about out the back door when her mother said, "We'll see you up there a little later."

What? There was no way her parents could be going to the Slush Cup. That was not part of her plan. She turned and tried to look as casual as possible.

"What do you mean you'll see me later?"

"At the hill," her dad said. "There'll be lots of people certainly, but I'm sure we'll see you up there."

"You're going?"

"Of course." Her mother laughed. "The whole town will be there. It's all anyone's talked about for months. Besides, now that your father is retiring, we're into trying new things."

Deanna didn't even want to consider what that comment might mean. Instead, she forced a smile and nodded. "Of course. Well, then I guess I'll see you up there."

She waited until she sat safely in the front seat of her car before she exhaled. It looked as if her day was about to get a whole lot more interesting. It was one thing to think of her parents finding out about her and Marcus from secondhand information. But it looked as if they were about to get a front row seat to her show.

BY MID-MORNING, the base of the hill was already packed with people. Marcus had run around all morning, fielding small crisis situations and more questions than he thought possible for one day. Despite a few minor hiccups with the sound system and a liftie who had shown up hungover, the day had come together quite well and by the excited crowd gathering around the slush pool, it was going to be a day for the record books.

The fact that he'd been so busy was probably a good thing because he hadn't had much time to think about Deanna. No, it was definitely a good thing. Because the little time he had thought about her had done nothing but get him distracted. And he'd have plenty of time to be distracted, later.

"You ready, buddy?" Malcolm appeared in the maintenance shed where Marcus was currently hiding out.

"I can't believe you're actually going to make me go through with this." Marcus still hadn't wrapped his head around the idea that he was about to board down a hill, off a ramp and into an icy, slushy pool. The whole thing was ridiculous. But if the amount of people outside ready to watch and the money from registrations that they were donating to the new foundation Kari Fox had set up for women in need was any indication, the general population didn't agree with him. The whole Slush Cup concept proved to be a whole lot more popular than he could have guessed.

"You owe me," Marcus said to his brother and gritted his teeth. "But I said I'd do it and I'm not going to back out now."

"Did you decide to go for a costume after all? I thought you were too cool for that." Malcolm pointed to the large duffle bag at Marcus's feet where he, in fact, did have a costume stored. But he wasn't about to tell his brother that.

"I guess you'll have to wait and see." He grabbed the straps of the bag and slung them over his shoulder, backpack style. "It's a surprise."

"Seriously? Just tell me it's cool."

Marcus laughed. "I assure you, it most certainly is *not* cool. But it is what it is and I was inspired." He grabbed his board and waved over his shoulder. "See you out there."

He had been inspired and only the day before. After spending his afternoon taking a few runs with his new buddy Dre, who'd continually called him the *King of the Board*, he'd decided that not only was he going to find a costume, he was going to make it memorable. And in a small town, with limited time, there weren't many options when it came to memorable costumes. Or costumes at all. But he did what he could.

He rode the chairlift up to the top of the hill, strapped his board on and took it easy as he made his way halfway down the hill. He knew exactly where he was going to go to change, and he made his way to the first-aid shack, which he knew would be empty. Marcus was right. The ski patrol was mostly all on duty down at the pool; unfortunately, that also meant he had to jimmy the lock open because he'd left his key chain in the maintenance shed, which he did with very little problem.

He could hear the announcer, Slade Black—the former lead singer of the Jacked Crackers, who had since started a solo career and had become a fixture in Cedar Springs since he fell in love with local Beth Martin—welcome the crowd to the festivities, an announcement which was met with a loud roar. No doubt the crowd would only get louder considering the beer gardens had only been open for an hour and Sam and Archer had been doing a swift business. There was something about a ski hill on a sunny day that went hand in hand with beer.

He would be up soon, so Marcus hurried and donned his costume before he tucked his duffle in the corner. He'd grab it later.

Back outside, he moved even faster. The sun might be shining, starting to melt the snow on the hill, but the breeze was still crisp, especially given the costume he'd chosen. He laughed at himself, knowing the reaction he was sure to get, and moved down into position at the start of the run.

He moved easily down the hill to the starting point where the crowd of participants had gathered, ready to compete for the variety of prizes that they'd put together. Seth, who was in charge of corralling the crazies—and they had to be crazy to volunteer for such a thing—took one look at Marcus and burst into laughter.

"Laugh it up." Marcus held his arms in the air and spun around on the board. "But I look damned good."

He wore only a bright blue lamé Speedo suit with a matching red and gold cape that flowed behind him, finished off with a shiny gold crown. It wasn't much, almost literally, but it was something. And if anything else, it would definitely be memorable. And that's what he was going for.

"You look...well, you certainly look..."

Marcus laughed. "That's the idea, right? Go big or go home?"

"Well, you might have your own opinions of big." Seth glanced down quickly and raised his brow.

"I don't think that's a problem."

"Save it for your girlfriend."

"What are you—right," Marcus recovered smoothly. "She has no complaints in that department." He grinned and donned his shades to keep from making eye contact. "Are we ready to do this?"

Seth gave him a weird look and turned his attention back down the hill, where Slade was getting the crowd going. "Right away. Let me check in."

"Let's speed this up. I'm freezing."

"That's nothing, buddy. Wait till you get in there. Did you test the waters before you came up?"

"I'd rather not know."

A voice came over the walkie-talkie; after a quick exchange, Seth looked up and patted Marcus on the back. "It's go time."

Marcus maneuvered his way through to the starting point, pulled his crown down tight on his head and as soon as he heard Slade announce, "The King of the Board," he held his hands in the air, muttered, "Here goes nothing," and started his descent.

Chapter Six

HER DAD HAD BEEN RIGHT. The entire town was up at Stone Summit for the Slush Cup. Deanna had to park at the far end of the lot and by the time she made her way through the half-melted slush and mud of the gravel parking lot, she'd worked up a bit of a sweat and wished she'd left her sweater, along with her jacket, in the car. She definitely needed a cold drink, which, from the looks of the crowd, wouldn't be a problem. It was easy to see the party atmosphere was in full swing in the ski village. Slade Black's voice boomed through the loudspeakers, the beer gardens were packed, and people everywhere laughed and had a great time.

She recognized a few people, but had no idea how she was going to find Marcus with so many people around. He'd texted her the night before to check that she was going to be there in order to *launch* their relationship. His word, not hers. Of course she was going to be there. Despite the butterflies she had doing cartwheels in her stomach all day, she was more than ready to get their little *relationship* going. The sooner, the better. But first she needed to find him. She stood on her tiptoes and tried to peer over the crowd, but there was no way she would find him that way.

Odds were good that he'd be somewhere close to the action considering he was working at the hill. From the sounds of it, he'd been pretty busy getting everything ready with Seth and Malcolm. She headed in the direction of the announcer's booth. Someone there was sure to know where he was; besides, the beer gardens were on the way. And a little bit of liquid courage couldn't hurt. She dropped her shoulder and navigated her way through the crowd.

Samantha and Archer were busy in the beer gardens, doing a swift business of cold drinks. Just to the side, a huge grill was set up where Samantha's husband, Trent, and his brother, Dylan, flipped burgers. They were all smiling and joking back and forth. Deanna felt a twinge of longing. They had such an easy friendship, as did almost all her old friends in Cedar Springs. She'd had it once, too. But not since she'd lived here. Toronto was different. A lot different. She missed that sense of belonging. Maybe if she—

"There you are." Cynthia appeared out of nowhere, grabbed her and spun her into a hug. "It's about time you showed up. We've been looking for you everywhere. But at least you didn't miss anything. Come on. You're just in time."

"I was just going to grab a beer."

"I have an extra one." Deanna turned to see Kylie, with two drinks in her hand. "I ordered two by instinct, but forgot about—" She gestured with her elbow to Cynthia's stomach and they all laughed.

"Seriously." Cynthia grabbed Deanna's hand. "We gotta go. I don't want to miss it."

"Miss what?" Deanna let herself be dragged along through the crowd, which seemed to magically part for Cynthia and Kylie.

"The whole reason we're here." Kylie laughed. "The Slush Cup. Remember?"

"Wait. That's really a thing? I thought it was just an excuse for a party."

"No way." Cynthia led them right up to a giant pool of water where there were bleachers set up. "This is totally a competition. Trust me. Seth hasn't shut up about it for months now. It's all he talks about. For real."

Deanna laughed. "Where is Seth?" She took a deep breath, avoided Kylie's eyes and added, "And Marcus. Do you know where Marcus is?"

Cynthia turned and stared at her. "Seriously? You don't know?"

"Know what?"

Beside her, Kylie laughed. "Come on. We better get to our seats." She led the way to the top of the bleachers, where a rope and a sign that read *Reserved* hung across the top row. "We know people." She winked and stepped over the rope. "Malcolm promised us the best seats."

Deanna settled in and looked out over the pool of water that appeared to have been dug into the snowbank. She still couldn't quite figure out the reason a ski hill would have a giant pool. Let alone one that looked to be filled with ice. But, she was willing to play along. "Okay," she said as Kylie handed her a beer. "Someone tell me the deal with the pool."

Sandwiched between both her friends, she was surrounded by their stares as they turned to face her. "Didn't Marcus tell you anything?" Cynthia demanded.

"You seriously don't know what this is about?"

"It's a party to celebrate the end of the season." Deanna shrugged and took a sip of her drink. The icy-cold drink was perfect, with the sun warming her face and the music blasting in the background. Sometimes a cold beer was the only choice.

"Well, it's totally a party," Cynthia said. "But it's going to be so much more than that. There are trophies involved."

"Trophies?"

"Oh yeah." Kylie and Cynthia both laughed and Deanna couldn't help but feel that she was missing the punch line on a joke, which obviously she was.

"Okay," she said slowly, because the girls didn't seem to want to tell her much more. "So you never said. Do you know where Marcus is?" She hated to ask, but at that point, she didn't think it would make much difference anyway.

Kylie and Cynthia exchanged glances. "Dee," Cynthia said. "Marcus is—"

Slade Black's voice over the announcement system interrupted her and they all stopped to listen.

"After a very successful first season, Stone Summit would like to welcome you to the first annual Slush Cup!"

The crowd cheered and Kylie held her beer up for clinking, which Deanna did and Cynthia joined in with her water bottle.

"For those of you who don't know how it's going to work today"— Cynthia looked in Deanna's direction—*"the competitors will all take turns skiing down the hill and flying into the pool."*

Deanna's mouth dropped open. On some level, she had to know that's what the pool was for, but still. It might be a warm day, but not warm enough for plunging into ice water.

"They will be judged in three different categories. Distance, style— because we like to see tricks." The crowd cheered again. *"And of course, costume choice."*

"Costume?"

Kylie laughed.

"Without further ado, let's get this party started!" Slade paused while the crowd around them roared. *"To kick off today's events, Stone Summit is honored to present the King of the Board."* Something twigged in Deanna's consciousness. She glanced at the girls, but their eyes were trained on the hill. The crowd hollered even

louder and when Slade announced his name, *"Marcus Stone, himself! And here he comes now,"* Deanna looked up, just in time to see Marcus, almost completely naked, carving down the hill on his board, a red cape flying out behind him.

Her hand flew to her mouth, but she couldn't seem to find any words as he got closer. Even from a distance, she could see his six-pack bunch and move in a fluid motion as he made his turns. Something inside her tightened and pulsed at the sight of his body. It had been years since she'd seen him without clothes and he was even more built than he was before. If it was even possible.

It was possible.

"Oh my God," Cynthia exclaimed. "Here he goes!"

As soon as the words were out of her mouth, Marcus hit the jump and with his arms outstretched over his head, executed a perfect summersault, let out a whoop and landed the jump on the surface of the water before unceremoniously splashing into the pool.

The crowd hooted and hollered, but Deanna let out a gasp. He'd hit hard. Too hard. And when he didn't surface right away, she jumped to her feet, her heart in her throat. She didn't stop and think, but ran down the bleacher steps to the orange snow fence barricade. Frantically, she tried to find a way through, but there was no give in the fence. Finally, she found a separation and pushed her body through to scramble up the snow to the edge of the pool.

She still couldn't see him. *Why wasn't anyone helping?* Deanna scanned the crowd, but no one seemed concerned.

"Marcus!" She pulled her sweater over her head, ready to dive into the icy waters herself, when the roar of the crowd got even louder. Instinctively, she looked to the left, and there he was, standing at the far end of the pool, arms thrust in the air, the stupid crown still affixed to his head—albeit slightly tilted now—grinning as if he'd just won the bloody Olympics.

Deanna sat back on her heels, pulled her sweater back into place and tried to control her growing anger. She'd been worried about him. Really worried. And he'd been fine. She felt like an ass as Marcus turned to encompass the whole crowd. When he finally looked in her direction, his smile froze momentarily as their eyes locked. She held her breath for a beat and he winked at her before she looked away.

DAMN, he was cold. No. He was freezing in a major shrinkage type of way. Not that he was thinking anything remotely sexual at the moment. All he was thinking of was getting some clothes on and getting some feeling back in his limbs. Then, maybe then, he would think about the look on Deanna's face when he saw her kneeling by the side of the pool. Oh, he'd think about it alright and he'd think about a whole lot more, too.

So much for not thinking anything sexual.

Marcus buttoned his jeans and pulled his t-shirt over his head, trying in vain to get the vision of Deanna out of his head. But it wasn't working. No, it was far from working. Up until the moment he'd locked eyes on her, he wasn't sure what her feelings for him really were. But there was no doubt now. None. Maybe it wasn't love, but there was definitely concern. It was clear now, more than ever, that even though she put on a tough act, there were at least some feelings there. Feelings he could definitely work with. A grin slid across his face, but he quickly wiped it when the door swung open.

"Dude! That was awesome."

"Hey." Marcus offered up his hand for a high five as Dre ran into the shed with the energy that only a thirteen-year-old boy had. "Did you like it?"

"Like it?" Dre slapped Marcus's hand. "You freakin' rocked. Your costume was perfect."

Marcus laughed. "It wasn't much of a costume." Marcus liked something about the kid and he'd hoped Dre would be impressed. "There were some pretty good ones out there."

"Yeah." Dre jumped up on the workbench and swung his legs, unable to stay still. "Did you see the chicken? That was epic. And the girl with the bikini—"

"Whoa. You shouldn't have seen that." It wasn't the bikini that Marcus objected to. After all, he'd worn pretty much the equivalent of a male bikini; it was the fact that the young woman in question had ripped her bikini top off moments before she went off the jump. It was definitely *not* family appropriate, but the crowd—largely, beer drinking men—had loved it. As had young Dre.

"Whatever," Dre said. "I wish I could see it again."

Marcus flicked his towel in the kid's direction and shook his head. "So are you going to hit the hill for one last run of the season?"

Dre shook his head. "Nah. I want to see who won the cup."

"Forget it." Marcus grabbed his sweater. "Forget it. That's lame. Go hit the hill, practice your skills. It's going to be a long summer with no boarding. Besides, the awards are being given out on the stage. I'm sure you'll hear it all from the hill. Slade's pretty loud."

"Slade Black, you mean?" Dre hopped off the bench. "You know him? Seriously, man. You're the coolest."

Marcus laughed and fought the urge to ruffle the kid's hair. He reminded him so much of himself at that age, it was crazy. "Come on. Maybe I'll introduce you to him a little later."

"For real?"

"But go get some boarding in. You'll regret it if you don't."

Dre nodded and Marcus had no doubt snowboarding would win over the draw of potentially seeing more women in bikinis on stage. And that was saying something for a teenage boy. But there was no doubt that boarding was Dre's passion. If he nurtured it, there was no telling where he'd end up.

"Will you come? Do a run with me?" Dre looked at him with so much hope in his eyes that for a second Marcus was tempted. But it was a big day and he had a lot to take care of still, not the least of which was finding Deanna Gordon.

"I wish I could, buddy. But I've got a list a mile long. Come on, I'll walk out with you."

The crowd had mostly dispersed away from the pool now that the actual jumping was over. Instead, they'd moved over to the stage where the band, the Jacked Crackers, was set to start performing soon. Crowds didn't bother Marcus anyway; he was used to them with all the traveling he'd done. He was also used to the group of people standing outside the door who waited for his autograph. He smiled and settled in easily to his snowboarding persona. He'd been off the circuit for a few months, but it wasn't long enough to forget this part of the job.

"Marcus!" A kid about Dre's age called for his attention. "Would you sign my board?" He handed Marcus a Sharpie pen.

"Absolutely. Are you going to compete when you're older?" Marcus scrawled his perfectly practiced signature.

"For sure. I'm going to the Olympics, man."

"Of course you are." He handed the pen back to the kid. "Good luck and keep riding."

Dre stood by his side while Marcus handled a half-dozen other requests for autographs and fielded questions about his return to the circuit. He didn't outright say he was going back, but he did leave the impression with his fans that there was a good chance. He still hadn't spoken to the reporter from *Shred* but he knew from experience that she could be anywhere, and he didn't want anything going to print that might harm his chances of a stellar return. If that's what he decided. An image of Deanna flashed in his mind to remind him where he needed to be. He'd invited her to the hill today and actually made a point via text message that she should be there to play the *good girlfriend* card. He better go find her before she changed her mind and took off.

"You need to get out on the hill, Dre. I've got work to do."

Dre kicked his boot into the snow. "But this is so cool."

"It'll never be you if you don't get some—"

"Marcus? Marcus Stone?"

Marcus and Dre turned together; Dre reacted first. "Whoa."

Marcus cuffed him on the back of his head, although he couldn't blame the kid for his frank reaction. The woman in front of him was gorgeous: tall, with long, blond hair that hung over her shoulders and teased the swell of her breasts. The very generous swell of her breasts. On their own accord, his eyes traveled the length of her and came back to rest on her full, very kissable red lips. "Excuse my friend here." Marcus extended his hand. "Marcus Stone. Would you like an autograph?"

"And where would you like to sign?" She put a hand on her hip and thrust her chest out. The very low v-neck shirt she wore left a very smooth, very exposed surface for Marcus to sign on and he gave her a sly grin.

"Well, there's a lot of—" Remembering a very young, very impressionable Dre stood next to him, he broke off that particular train of thought. He glanced down at the kid, and then up again. But instead of his eyes landing on the blond, they locked on another very beautiful, albeit very pissed-off woman a little farther away.

Deanna.

Marcus forced an innocent smile on his face and tried to indicate with his eyes that he'd only be a moment, but Deanna turned and walked away.

Dammit. Now he'd have to go find her again.

"I actually don't want an autograph," the blond said and refocused his attention. "My name is April Easton. I'm from *Shred* magazine. Can we go somewhere private and talk?" It was probably an innocent question, but coming out of April's mouth, it was anything but innocent. Marcus had no doubt about where that particular conversation would be headed. A month ago, he might have considered it. Hell, a week ago he might have. But things were different now.

"How about we answer a few questions right here and I can introduce you to my brother, Malcolm? He owns the hill." With only a slight bit of guilt, Marcus added, "We're identical twins." He knew by saying it he would likely be misleading April in all kinds of ways, but Malcolm was a big boy; he could handle it.

April only looked slightly disappointed, but she pulled out a recorder and clicked it on. "Sure. That would be okay, I guess."

"Great, let's walk and talk." Aware that Dre still trailed behind him, Marcus headed in the direction where Deanna had disappeared. "Let's get started."

"No problem." April switched easily from sex kitten groupie into reporter and started to sling questions at him. The first few were pretty basic, and Marcus was able to answer them with the well-scripted answers he usually used. Which was a good thing, because he was totally preoccupied looking for Deanna, who had completely disappeared into the crowd. It was going to be pretty hard to be her *boyfriend*—even if it was imaginary—if they weren't seen together.

"So can we expect to see you back on the circuit next season?"

Marcus paused at the question. His answer should have come easily, but something stopped him.

"Well?"

Marcus swallowed and gave April his most charming smile. "Well, I'd like to say yes, April," he started. "But there's got to be a little bit of mystery, too, don't you think?" He winked, but April didn't give.

"What about the new extreme boarding film that's scheduled to start production?" she asked. "Rumor has it you've been flagged as a favorite to star. Will you be joining the crew in Europe for the start of filming next month?"

Right then, Marcus caught sight of Deanna with a group of their friends. Their eyes connected. He gave her a sexy smile and without looking back to April, said, "Nothing's been signed yet, April. But when there is, you'll be the first to know about it. There's Malcolm, now. Let me introduce you and then if you have any more questions later, I'd be happy to answer them."

Once the quick introductions were made, Marcus was able to slip away and turn his attention to Deanna.

She looked fantastic, and that heat in his groin that he'd felt earlier was back. She wore simple leggings and a long sweater, but damn, he couldn't remember the last time he'd seen a woman more beautiful. Deanna had a classic, easy beauty and even with the oversized sweater, Marcus could clearly see the dip of her waist and the swell of her ass that he used to love running his hands over.

The thought of having his hands on those curves again, even for a minute, made his blood run hot and his cock twitch.

As if she could feel his eyes on her, she turned and looked over her shoulder at him. The corner of her mouth curled up into a half smile, which he found encouraging. The fun was just getting started.

"Showtime," he mouthed and closed the distance between them.

DEANNA WASN'T sure what she'd expected when Marcus

finally joined her, but she wasn't totally prepared for the heat of his arm as it slid around her waist as he tugged her gently into him. "Hey," he whispered in her ear. "It's about time I found you."

Her first reaction had been to shrug his arm off her and she was about to object that she hadn't been hiding at all, but she caught herself just in time. They were supposed to be a couple, after all, and besides that, his arm felt kind of nice.

"I've been around." She tried to keep her voice light. "It's you who's been busy. Flying through the air in your underwear, no less."

"You liked that, did you?"

To her annoyance, a flush crept over her cheeks. "It's not that I—"

"Is she your girlfriend?"

Without removing his arm, Marcus spun them so they faced a teenage boy she'd never seen before. "Aren't you on the hill yet?"

"I'm going, I'm going," the kid said. "But is she?"

Deanna looked to Marcus for some sort of explanation, which he provided. "Deanna, this is Dre. Dre, Deanna."

"Your girlfriend?"

It was their first test as a couple and sure, it was from a kid, but it still felt monumental when Marcus said, "Yes. Deanna is my girlfriend." A chill ran through her, mostly because the words didn't sound nearly as foreign as she expected they would, and Marcus squeezed her quickly. Maybe he felt it too? She didn't have time to dwell on that thought, which was definitely a good thing, because Dre stuck his hand out.

She took it and shook it, noting his firm grip. "It's nice to meet you, Dre." Deanna shook his hand and smiled at Cynthia, who'd just joined the group. "Have you guys been friends long?" She'd always liked kids, and something about Dre made her smile.

"Just since yesterday," he said very seriously. "But Marcus is kinda like my mento."

"Your mento?"

"I think you mean mentor," Marcus said. "And I guess I am. I showed Dre some moves yesterday. It was cool."

It was cool, but Deanna didn't say anything. She had no idea Marcus was good with kids. It was oddly attractive. Not that she wanted to be attracted to him. Not anymore than she already was. But that was just a physical thing; it was normal and natural because after all, Marcus was hot. She could deal with that. However, she didn't need any reason to be attracted to Marcus in any other way. Their arrangement was just that. An arrangement.

"I helped him, too." Dre's face filled with pride. "The costume was my idea. Right, Marcus?"

Deanna looked at him with raised eyebrows. The costume, or lack thereof, was the idea of a teenage boy? Interesting.

Marcus pulled his arm away, a loss she felt at once. "It wasn't totally his idea." He tucked his hands in his back pockets.

"But I called you the King of the Board, remember?"

Dre looked like he might get upset, and to his credit, Marcus noticed, too. "It's true," he admitted. "You called me that."

"And that's where the costume came from, right?" There was so much hope in the boy's face that Deanna silently willed Marcus to agree with him, even if it wasn't true.

To her relief, Marcus nodded. "Actually," he said, "that's exactly where the idea came from. Although I was hoping to get a costume with a bit more...coverage."

"Your costume?" That blond appeared from out of nowhere again. She thrust her breasts out in Marcus's direction, and Deanna had to fight the urge to poke them to see if they'd deflate. Instead, she sucked in her stomach and tried to stand a little taller. There was nothing quite like a real-life Barbie doll to make a girl feel insecure. "I thought it was perfect," the blond cooed.

"My name is Dresden Diamond." Dre pushed himself between the woman and Marcus, and Deanna's opinion of him rose even higher. "But you can just put me down as Dre. I'm going to be the next Marcus Stone." He spun to look at Marcus. "Right?"

Marcus nodded and laughed. "He is. Especially if he gets out and practices."

"I'm going. I'm going." Dre turned back to the reporter. "It's D-R-E-S—"

"I got it." She clicked off her recorder. "You know what? I have a few more questions for Malcolm." With a swish of her blond hair, she was gone, and Deanna rolled her eyes at her departing back.

"What was that for?"

She blinked hard and looked at Marcus, who'd caught her out. "Nothing."

"Right."

"Was it something I said?" Dre asked. "She didn't seem to like me."

"That's just how she is. Now you are going to have to excuse me, though, buddy. I'm going to have to spend a little time with my woman here."

Dre smiled as if he knew what Marcus was talking about, which would have been impressive considering Deanna barely knew. "Gotcha. I'll catch up with you later. See ya, Deanna." With a wave and a bounce that quickly turned into an attempted swagger or a kid trying to figure himself out, he was gone.

"Nice kid."

"He is." Marcus stared at her, his eyes boring into her.

"What?" She shook her head and tried to look away.

He ignored her. "Got a little jealous there, did you?" He slid his arm around her waist again and despite herself, Deanna found herself wanting to melt into him and let his strong arms hold her close the way they had so many years ago. Instead, she tried to pull away.

But Marcus only tightened his grip. "Where do you think you're going?"

"You don't have to—"

"On the contrary." He pulled her closer and whispered in her ear as if they really were lovers. "If we're going to pull this off, don't you think we're going to have to actually look like we like each other?"

"It's not that I don't like you," she objected quickly and without thinking.

"Oh yeah? Could've fooled me." He grinned wickedly, and it sparked something low in her belly. *Damn, his smile always got her.* "Isn't that why you left?"

His comment hit her hard. Deanna exhaled slowly. "It's complicated, Marcus," she whispered. "This isn't the time or—"

"What are you two talking about over there?" Cynthia called out. "It looks serious and this is a party. Come on, we're about to toast to the first year of Stone Summit."

With an ease that came way too casually to him, Marcus smiled. "Ready, babe?" And before waiting for an answer, he steered her toward the group where plastic glasses were pressed into their hands and toasts were made.

As Deanna raised her glass and clinked with everyone, her eyes swept past Kylie. She couldn't help but notice the other woman watched her with a look she couldn't quite read. There was no way Kylie still had any lingering feelings for Marcus. That was ancient history. And there was no way she could know the truth about Deanna and Marcus and what they were trying to pull off. Deanna smiled sweetly at

Kylie, who paused for a moment before she returned the smile.

No. It couldn't be any of those things. Kylie was probably just curious like the rest of their friends about the sudden relationship between the two of them. The now familiar feeling of guilt returned at the idea that they were lying to everyone, but Deanna pushed it away just as she had been doing. It wouldn't matter how she accomplished her task of getting out of Cedar Springs. Just that she did it.

Chapter Seven

MARCUS MANAGED to finish his interview with April Easton without any more drama, not least of which was giving her the impression that he was interested in hooking up with her. In the past, absolutely. But not now. He couldn't explain it, but something had shifted. The thought of a one-night stand with a gorgeous blond just wasn't that appealing. If any of his buddies ever heard him say anything like that, they'd never believe it. But it was true. He hated even thinking it, but the only woman he was even remotely attracted to at the moment currently stood next to the stage, her arms over her head as she cheered for the band to come out.

Spending the day with Deanna and pretending to be her boyfriend had been way easier than he'd thought. He'd spent the night before worried about looking forced and having one of their friends call them on their story. But it hadn't been that way at all. It had been easy—too easy—to fall into a comfort-able rhythm with her. Sure, it had only been for a day, but they were more than pulling it off. He needed to be careful and remind himself that it wasn't real.

He had one goal with Deanna: to break her heart the way she'd broken his.

It sounded worse than it was. At least that's what he kept telling himself. And he'd keep telling himself that, too. Whatever it took. But one thing was certain. If things felt this good between them after only one day, he would not be able to survive too much of this charade without risking his own heart. And that was the last bloody thing he needed. No, he better kick things up into high gear and get it over with as soon as possible.

When he spotted a few familiar faces in the crowd, he got the perfect idea of how to do that.

"Mr. Gordon." He slapped the man on the back so he spilled his drink. Jim turned and gave Marcus a brief scowl.

"It's Dr. Gordon, son."

"Right." He nodded at Deanna's mother. "Gayle." The woman's jaw flexed and tensed. No doubt she bit her tongue to keep from correcting him to address her properly. Deanna's parents were very old school, and although the doctor had been able to cover up his general dislike of him, his wife never had. Marcus swallowed hard and forced a grin. If they hadn't liked him before, they really weren't going to like him in a few minutes.

"Nice to see people of your age up here today. We're really excited about how the day is going."

"People of our age?"

He hated being an ass, but it went with the territory. "Well, what I meant, was, the Jacked Crackers usually capture a younger audience, but of course it's nice to see the whole town here today."

"Of course." Dr. Gordon nodded tersely.

Gayle turned away from him altogether and he went in for the kill. "Have you seen your beautiful daughter yet? There are so many people I know, it's hard to keep track of anyone."

Gayle answered. "We haven't. But she's probably busy with friends and she was going to the clinic beforehand. She works very hard, our girl."

"Don't I know it?" Marcus nodded and gave her a wink; the older woman blushed. "I know where she is if you want to say hi."

Gayle perked up and scanned the crowd. "That might be nice."

With a jerk of his head, Marcus walked and moved quickly through the crowd. He reached Deanna first and without hesitation wrapped his arms around her waist. He had a fraction of a second to register the fact that she didn't tense up the way she had earlier, but melted into his touch easily. He whispered in her ear. "It's time to take this up a notch."

She whipped around to look at him but before she could say anything, Marcus captured her mouth and those luscious lips into a kiss. She tasted just as sweet as he remembered. More so. It only took her a second to respond to him, and when she did, he deepened the kiss, threading his hand up to the back of her head, and held her to him. She was so damn responsive to him, there was a heat low in his belly and there was no doubt that if they kept at it too much longer, he'd need some kind of release.

The part of his brain that processed logic knew it wasn't real. The kiss, just like everything else, had been executed for a specific purpose, but he didn't care. He was going to enjoy every moment of having her in his arms again. But the sound of a throat clearing behind him reminded him of where he was and what exactly he was doing.

Deanna pulled away, but not before Marcus sucked her bottom lip into his mouth and gave it a gentle nip. Her face was flushed, her lips swollen like a woman who'd just been thoroughly kissed, which she most certainly had been. But when she saw who stood behind Marcus, her beautiful dark eyes grew wide.

"Mom. Dad." Even in the dim lighting, it was easy to see her flush grew deeper. "What are you doing here?"

Marcus recovered quickly and slipped easily into his role, sliding his arm around her and pulling her close. The tension from earlier was back and Deanna held herself stiffly next to him, so he squeezed a little tighter to keep her from running away.

"We told you we were coming up today," her father answered. "I...we..." He looked to Gayle. "Didn't expect that...well, that," he gestured in Marcus's direction, "you were seeing anyone."

"Oh...I'm not—"

"Not sure how it happened so fast," Marcus cut her off and finished easily. "When I saw Deanna again after all those years, there was just something about her that I couldn't resist. And she couldn't seem to resist me either—could you, pumpkin?"

She stared at him and blinked slowly before a very forced smile crossed her face. "It's true. How could you resist his charm?"

"So you're...together?" Gayle swallowed hard, as if she found the very idea of them together distasteful, which she probably did. Damn, maybe Deanna was right and they really hated him enough that they'd rather she go back to Toronto than stay around him. Sure, she'd said as much. That was the whole reason for what they were doing, but he hadn't really believed it. Not really.

They all waited for Deanna to answer her mother's question. It had to be her who answered because when she did, it would confirm everything. Finally, she nodded. "We are," she said. "And I think it's serious."

"Serious?" Dr. Gordon sputtered. "But you only just started dating. You didn't mention anything about this before. How could it possibly be serious? This is a man who just wore underwear in front of the entire town, Deanna. Be serious."

Marcus clenched his jaw. "It was a costume, Dr. Gordon. For the event. I don't normally wear that type of thing." He couldn't believe he was actually defending himself against the type of judgment that was completely unfounded and downright discriminatory, but there was no way he would stand there and let that man disrespect him. Show or not.

The doctor ignored him, and turned back to his daughter. "We'll have to talk about this later."

He knew how much it cost her, but Deanna put a smile on her face and shook her head. "There's nothing really to talk about, Dad." The crowd around them roared to life. "The show's starting." And just like that, the Jacked Crackers appeared on stage in a flash of lights and sound; the concert started and drowned out any further discussion. With one last glance toward the doctor and his wife, who stood among the crowd, shell-shocked that their perfect daughter had just hooked up with the town playboy, he wrapped his arms around his fake girlfriend and gave her a kiss on the neck before he whispered in her ear. "Nicely done, babe."

DEANNA HAD NEVER BEEN MORE grateful for a distraction as when the band started to play. It was the perfect excuse to turn away and ignore her parents, even if she felt like a terrible daughter for doing it. Who was she kidding? She *was* being a terrible daughter. Lying, manipulating: she didn't do those things. Or at least, she never had before.

Marcus tightened his arms around her waist and despite the fact that she knew it was a show and none of it was real, his arms felt good. Really good. As had the kiss. Her body trembled involuntarily, just thinking about the way his lips on hers had lit her up. How was it even possible to respond to him so readily after so much time had passed? She'd assumed their connection was dead, but if that kiss was any indication, it was anything but.

She allowed herself to get lost in the music and tuned out every other negative feeling that kept trying to push in. She steadfastly avoided looking to the left, where her parents had been standing. If she knew them at all, they would have retreated to the sidelines to watch the show. Although the fact that they were at the show at all still shocked her. Maybe she didn't know them as well as she'd thought. No. She pushed that idea away. They'd reacted to Marcus just as she knew they would. There may have been some changes, but as far as their little girl was concerned, her mom and dad were still the same.

After a few songs, Marcus yelled so she could hear. "Let's grab a drink."

She nodded and took his hand as if it was the most natural thing in the world and he led her through the crowd to the tables they'd reserved for the night. There were a few faces she recognized from the past and she greeted her old friend Rhys Anderson, who was now one of the sheriffs in town, with a big hug before he introduced her to his girlfriend, Kari. Marcus disappeared to grab some drinks and she was introduced to Bria Sheridan and Jax Carver, who both seemed to be great people and fit into the crowd perfectly. Deanna couldn't help but wonder whether she still fit into the crowd and normally, she would have held herself back a little, but she was so caught up in the party atmosphere, and the few drinks she'd had, that she stopped herself from overthinking anything, and just jumped in to the conversations that were going on around her.

"It's so good to see you again, Dee," Beth Martin said. "And you're so successful. You make us all proud." She hadn't seen Beth in years, and to find out she had a teenage daughter and was now engaged to superstar Slade Black blew her mind.

"Me? You're the one about to marry a rock star. I'm just a doctor. Have you guys set a date yet?"

Beth smiled and looked over to Slade, who was deep in conversation with the men. "Actually, we finally nailed down a date last night."

"Last night?" Sam joined them. "This one's for real, right?" Sam and Beth were best friends and only the Christmas before, Beth had helped Sam's husband pull off the ultimate surprise, pretending she and Slade were getting married at the romantic Castle Mountain Lodge, when really he'd pulled off a surprise wedding for Sam.

Beth laughed. "I promise this one is real. But it is going to be kind of fast."

"What do you consider fast?"

Beth grinned. "You have to promise to keep it quiet," she said. "We're trying to squeeze it in before Slade goes on tour and we really don't want the press to find out. It was bad enough with the engagement and—"

"Beth! When is it?" Samantha demanded.

"In two weeks."

Deanna almost choked. "Two weeks? Is it even possible to plan a wedding that fast?" She looked over at Sam, who just smiled.

"Well, I did it," Sam said. "When I thought it was for her. I'm sure we can pull it off." She pulled her best friend in for a hug. "It's about time we had another wedding in town anyway. Anything I can do to help, let me know."

Deanna raised her eyebrow, but Sam missed it. Sam was supposed to be reducing stress, not adding to it. She had noticed that the other woman sipped water instead of the beer she'd been serving, but still, if she wanted to increase her chances of conception, she'd really need to relax a little.

"Hey girls." Kylie and Cynthia joined the group and slipped into seats across from them. It was probably her imagination, but Deanna could have sworn that Kylie was doing her best to avoid looking at her. The knot of guilt tightened in her chest. She was going to have to tell Kylie the truth about what had happened years ago. But then again, what was one more lie on top of everything else?

"Are you all having fun?" Cynthia asked. "It's a great party, isn't it?"

"I can't believe you're out there dancing," Beth said. "When I was pregnant with Jules, I was so tired all the time."

"I was," Cynthia said. "And so sick, too. But let me tell you, the second trimester is amazing. I have so much energy and my sex drive! I can't get—"

"Okay," Kylie interrupted. "I don't think we need to talk about this right now. The guys are probably listening."

The women all slipped into easy conversation full of laughter and excitement over Beth's coming nuptials and Deanna found herself sucked into the circle of friendship. She hadn't realized how much she'd missed the closeness of other women, but it was nice. Really nice.

After a few minutes, the men joined them and Marcus slid his hands over her shoulders; one hand trailed slowly down the side of her neck. She knew he was only doing it as part of their act, but her body would need to be reminded of that fact because it reacted instantly with a deep ache in her core. If they hadn't been in public, she wasn't sure she'd be able to be trusted with the feelings he was sparking in her body. *Of course, if we weren't in public, it wouldn't be happening at all*, she reminded herself.

"I assume my beautiful bride told you all the news." Slade kissed Beth on the cheek. "I hope you'll all be there."

"Of course."

"Wouldn't miss it."

A chorus of exclamations went up around the table.

Deanna smiled. A wedding would be fun. If she was still in

town. A lot could happen in two weeks. If everything went according to plan, she could be back in Toronto by then. The smile fell off her face and she looked down momentarily. The idea of not being at the wedding bothered her more than it should have. She needed to stay strong and stop letting feelings get in her way. She looked up and met Kylie's unsmiling gaze.

"Is everything okay, Dee?" Kylie asked.

"I was going to ask you the same thing." Deanna thought quickly. "You must be thinking of your own wedding. I can't believe how many of you are planning weddings right now."

"There's really only two of us," Kylie answered seriously. "And Malcolm and I aren't worrying about picking a date yet. I still have to finish school."

"Of course." Deanna forced a smile and tried to turn away.

"You know," Kylie said, "I still can't quite wrap my head around the two of you together." She nodded toward Marcus, who still stood behind her and played with her hair, which made it very hard to concentrate. "There's something not quite right about it."

"What do you mean?" Deanna tried to make her voice sound light, but she was fairly sure she didn't succeed. "What could possibly not be right?"

"There's a lot right about this." Marcus dropped to her neck and sucked the sensitive skin into his mouth. Deanna had to work hard to keep from moaning. She'd never been one for a public display of affection before, but then again, she'd never really had the opportunity to have any public displays of affection. "I'm going to steal my woman away for the last dance."

Deanna noticed then that the band had started to play their current number-one ballad, "Run Away With Me." "I love this song," she said.

"Good. Let's dance."

AS THERE WAS no official dance floor, Marcus led her to a somewhat empty spot on the floor, where he spun her into his arms. She fit so damn perfectly. Playing her boyfriend was easy. Too easy, but he might as well enjoy it. He let one hand slide down her back to the swell of her ass where he left it before he tilted her face up to his. He stroked her cheek with his thumb. "So you were pretty jealous earlier." He grinned.

"What are you talking about?" She tilted her head slightly to the side, so his hand slipped from her cheek. He ran the back of his fingers down her neck instead.

"Earlier, with the reporter," he teased. "You were jealous."

"No I wasn't."

"You were."

"It doesn't matter. You can sleep with whoever you want." She wouldn't look at him.

Marcus cupped her chin so she wouldn't be able to look away. "It does matter. I'm your boyfriend."

"Not—"

He silenced her with a finger on her lips and a smile. "It's going pretty well, don't you think?"

"Very well," she said with a sexy smile. Marcus couldn't tell whether it was the effect of the alcohol, or whether she was just playing her role too damned well, but there was heat in her eyes. "It's kind of fun, too, don't you think?" She licked her lips in a way that made his cock thicken in his pants and he pulled her tighter to him. If she was playing a game with him, he'd be the first to let her know he'd come to play. By the way she gasped, he knew she could feel exactly what kind of effect she had on him.

They swayed in time to the music, the friction between their bodies building. "They're all probably watching us," Marcus said without taking his eyes off hers.

"Good. That's the idea, right? They're supposed to believe we're really a couple."

"Well then, we better make sure they do."

"What do you mean?"

"A real boyfriend wouldn't think twice about copping a feel." His left hand squeezed her ass and cupped the delicious flesh in his hand; she gasped and jumped a little. Marcus used the opportunity to pull her even closer up against his throbbing core. "And a real boyfriend would have no problem about showing his girlfriend exactly how hot and bothered she was making him." He knew it was a risk, but he took Deanna's hand and slid it down between their bodies so it rested over the bulge in his jeans. He half expected her to jerk away from her and slap him, but he also knew she wouldn't do anything to risk blowing their cover, so he took full advantage of it.

She narrowed her eyes at him, but they were full of heat. "That was bold."

"Just trying to keep it real." He grinned wickedly, but when she squeezed his crotch, he thought he might come totally undone right there in the crowd. Maybe pushing the limits with her wasn't such a good idea after all. "Okay." He moved her hand away. "You made your point."

"Did I? Because I was just getting started." She crushed her lips to his and all at once, the line between what was real and what was fake blurred as she kissed him with a hunger he vividly remembered. Greedily, he kissed her back. Fake or not, the heat of her mouth on his felt damned real.

"Hey." From somewhere behind him, Marcus heard his brother, but he ignored him in favor of the delicious woman in his arms. "Marcus. Come up for air already. The concert's over."

Reluctantly, Marcus pulled away from Deanna. She looked at him with so much need in her eyes and her chest heaved in a way that made her breasts strain against her tight t-shirt; he contemplated ignoring his twin again in favor of another kiss. Or more.

"What?" he finally asked Malcolm.

Malcolm grinned at him and laughed. "I'm pretty sure the two of you didn't notice, but the concert is over. Time to go."

Slowly, Marcus looked around at the thinning crowd. The security crew they'd hired ushered everyone to the exits. Just like that, the Slush Cup was over and it had been a success. "I can't believe it's over already."

"Well, you were pretty occupied," Malcolm said. "Come on. We're going to have one more celebratory drink while we're waiting to close up."

He slipped his hand in Deanna's and they followed his brother back to the table where a bottle of champagne and a fresh set of plastic glasses were laid out. "I couldn't find any champagne flutes," Seth apologized. "And I got you apple juice, Cyn." He kissed his girlfriend on the cheek.

"This is great." Malcolm grabbed the bottle. Everyone else had disappeared, leaving just the six of them to celebrate together. "I really wanted a private celebration with you all who really helped me make this happen this year."

Marcus glanced over at Deanna, who looked at her feet. It was true that she hadn't had anything to do with Stone Summit, but as Marcus's *girlfriend*, Malcolm had graciously included her. No doubt she felt out of place. Marcus wrapped his arm around her shoulder and pulled her into his side. She gave him a grateful smile and he nodded simply before he turned back to Malcolm.

"This has been one hell of a year," Malcolm said. "And I never could have done it without you guys. Seth, thank you for being my right-hand man. I know I left you with a lot on your plate, and you more than rose to the occasion. The Slush Cup was a great idea, and the perfect way to close out the season. Good job, man." Seth nodded and Marcus was only slightly chapped that his twin brother had referred to someone else as his *right hand*. But then it was Marcus's turn. "And you, brother. I still don't really know why you decided to leave the circuit and—"

"Take a break," Marcus interjected.

Malcolm raised an eyebrow in question, but continued. "Okay, I don't know why you decided to take a break from the circuit, but I'm glad you did. We needed you this year and there's no doubt that you were crucial to pulling this whole thing off. And hey, it's good to have family in high places. The media coverage from today will be huge for early season pass sales for next year."

Marcus nodded. He knew it was his name that had brought the media coverage, and if it helped Stone Summit, it was fine by him.

"Okay, enough talking already," Kylie said. "Let's drink."

Everyone laughed, but Malcolm wasn't done. "I haven't toasted you yet," he said to her. They shared a private moment, just looking at each other, and Marcus felt the familiar twinge of wishing he had what his brother had. Deanna nuzzled a little closer to him, and something in his stomach flipped. Maybe he did have it and he just didn't know it?

No.

He couldn't risk thinking that way. Not for one second. It was way too dangerous. Besides, after only one good day between them—even if it wasn't fake—it was too fast. *But everything with Deanna had always been fast.*

"You don't need to toast me, hon. I know exactly what I mean to you because it's exactly the same thing you mean to me."

"Awwww," Cynthia said. "You guys are too cute."

"Enough already." Seth reached for the bottle. "If you're not going to open that, I am. I have to get my baby mama home to bed."

"Right." Malcolm turned and kept the bottle from Seth's reach. "And I need to get my fiancée home to my bed."

All eyes turned to Marcus and Deanna, no doubt waiting for Marcus to say something similar. And he would have, too. But they hadn't talked about what to do. Of course, after the way they were just making out on the dance floor, it might look a little strange if Marcus went home alone while Deanna returned to her parents' house. "I don't think I need to tell anyone that I'm anxious to get Dee alone." He felt her stiffen next to him, and he squeezed her arm in an effort to reassure her, but she didn't relax. It didn't matter. They'd figure it out.

DEANNA SIPPED the champagne she'd toasted with, feeling more than a little like an imposter. Of course, that's what she was. An imposter. She had no business being part of their celebration. The last thing she needed was anything else to drink. Not that she'd had much. A few beers earlier in the day and then nothing till the champagne: she was definitely not tipsy, but maybe it would be better if she was. The whole day had been crazy.

Fun. But crazy.

Pretending with Marcus had actually been a lot of fun, especially the kiss. But every once in a while, the reality of what they were doing and what she was playing at smacked her in the face. Like when Marcus had just more or less announced that he couldn't wait to be alone with her. Sure, they'd been going at it pretty hot and heavy on the dance floor, but that had all been for show. *Hadn't it?* The heat in her belly and the dampness in her panties had definitely been real, as had the hard bulge in Marcus's pants. But that didn't mean anything.

Or did it?

She couldn't dwell on it. The day had been great, but also

more than a little confusing. She'd never expected her feelings to be so conflicted. It was supposed to be clear-cut, but what she felt was anything but clear. She needed to sleep. Everything would look different in the morning.

"So, where are you guys going?" Kylie asked as they finished their drinks.

Deanna stared at her, not sure she understood the question. "Pardon me?"

"Where are you going?" Kylie asked again. "I mean, tonight." Something in Kylie's eyes put Deanna on guard. "Marcus just said he wanted to be alone with you. Where's that going to be? I assume you're not going to take him home to your house. I'm sure your mom and dad wouldn't like that."

Her tone was borderline bitchy, but there was no way Deanna would call her on it. At least not yet. She needed to get her old friend alone to figure out what was going on with her. Besides, Kylie had a point. Marcus had declared that they needed to be alone together. But what did that mean? He was living with Malcolm, and Kylie was staying there now as well after giving up her apartment down in town. There was no way in hell she was taking him home to her house. Hell, she wasn't taking him home at all. It was a fake relationship. They couldn't go home together. That was ridiculous.

"Actually." Deanna looked at Marcus for help and tried to think fast. "I have an early meeting."

"She's coming home with me."

They spoke at the same time and it took a second for Deanna to register what Marcus had said. "Pardon?"

"You don't have a meeting on Sunday, babe," Marcus said smoothly. "You'll come with me."

Deanna could feel her cheeks fill with heat. "But I'm sure that Malcolm and Kylie want to—"

"But that's where I'm staying." Marcus shrugged. "I'm sure they won't mind."

Malcolm laughed and wrapped his arm around Kylie. "Not at all," he said. "Just be sure to keep it down."

Oh my God, he didn't just say that. Deanna thought she was going to die from embarrassment. There was no way they could go through with this. She needed to get Marcus alone and talk to him, but that opportunity didn't come until they'd cleared the rest of the champagne and said good-bye to Seth and Cynthia, who headed home.

"I just need to grab something from the office," Malcolm said. "If you want to wait, we can all walk back together."

Marcus nodded, but the second Malcolm and Kylie disappeared inside, Deanna spun to face him. "We can't do this," she hissed. "I can't spend the night with you. What will my parents think?"

"Exactly what you want them to." He smiled confidently.

He had a point.

"What about us? I mean, this isn't—"

"Look," he said. "It's all part of the show, right?" She felt a pinch of disappointment at his words. "I'll be a perfect gentleman." He threaded his fingers through hers and brought her hand up to his mouth. "Unless you don't want me to.

Chapter Eight

"HERE. YOU CAN WEAR THIS." Marcus handed her one of his old boarding t-shirts. "Make yourself at home."

Deanna lingered near the door to his bedroom for a moment longer, before she crossed the floor to take the shirt. "Thanks."

"There are spare toothbrushes in the second drawer," he added. "Malcolm's very organized for guests. Too bad I've been occupying his guest room for the last few months." He tried to joke, but he only managed a small smile out of her. "Do you want a snack or anything? I can—"

"I'm actually pretty tired." She moved for the adjoining bathroom. "I'm just going to go..."

"Right."

As soon as she closed the door behind her, Marcus fell backward on the bed and let out a sigh of frustration. For years he'd dreamed about having Deanna in his bed again. He'd lain awake too many nights to count and thought of her killer curves and his mouth kissing his way down them to find the sweetness between her legs. And now she was here. In his bedroom. And he was going to spend the night torturously close to her, but he couldn't touch her.

No. Scratch that. He could. If she wanted him to. And maybe that wasn't as big of an *if* as he thought. Her body had responded just as readily to their make-out session on the dance floor as his had. No, it wouldn't be a stretch of the imagination to find that she wanted him just as badly. But how far was she willing to take this little charade of hers? And more importantly, how willing was he to risk his heart again?

No. That wouldn't be an issue. He was a different man now. Wiser, hardened. And going in with both eyes open. Wide open.

The door creaked as Deanna stepped out of the bathroom. With an easy crunch, he sat up on the bed. "Hey."

Damn. He shouldn't have looked. She'd let her long, thick hair out of the braid it had been restrained in and was laid in waves over her shoulder. His fingers itched to plow through that mass of hair and use it to tug her to him. Marcus stifled a groan as his eyes traveled down her body. She filled out his old shirt better than he ever could have imagined. No, scratch that; she filled it out better than his wildest dreams about her, and there had been dreams. Too many to count.

Despite the loose fabric, her large, full breasts were perfectly silhouetted. His eyes traveled over both luscious curves before falling to where the hem of cotton ended, mid-thigh. *Hell.* If she so much as took a step, the material would ride up and he'd see her panties. *Take a step*, he silently urged. "Did you find everything okay?" he asked as soon as he trusted his voice.

She nodded and bit her bottom lip, an action that caused his dick to stiffen painfully in his jeans. Damn. The woman drove him to the brink. She'd always had that effect on him. From the first time they'd met, he'd needed her in a bad way and once hadn't been enough with her. It had never been enough. Watching her now, as she made her way slowly to the bed—there was a flash of red panties visible, just as he thought, when she moved—he had the sinking feeling that it would never be enough when it came to Deanna. The only cure was to stay strong. *Compartmentalize, Stone,* he commanded himself.

"Is this side of the bed okay?"

She was being so shy, so proper. He couldn't stand it.

"No."

"Okay." She halted before she sat on the bed and moved to the opposite side, but she stopped herself. "I just realized something."

That you're the sexiest woman to ever walk the earth? "What's that?"

"I have no idea what side of the bed you sleep on." She spoke matter-of-factly, but he could see the confession bothered her. "I mean, after everything...all we had..." She shook her head. "It doesn't matter, really. I just realized that this is the first time we've actually spent the night together and considering our past, it's kind of strange, don't you think?"

It was strange, but so was their past relationship. They'd been sneaking around, and their entire relationship—if that's what you could even call it—was based on dishonesty, so all they'd had were stolen moments: Quickies in his truck. A few heated rendezvous at the natural spring pools on the mountainside. And one night when her parents had been out, a particularly memorable time in her childhood bed. But Deanna was right; they'd never spent the whole night together. Despite the strong feelings he had for her, he'd never held her in his arms and inhaled the scent of her shampoo as she slept. They'd never shared that intimacy. The thought struck him, but he shrugged in an effort to play it off. "I suppose you're right."

She looked a little sad as she moved again. "It seems a little odd that now that we're just pretending to be together, we get to have that moment, is all. I always thought it would be special to spend the night with a guy."

"Wait." All Marcus's senses were on high alert. "What do you mean, you've always thought? You've never spent the entire night with a man?" He found the idea hard to believe. Very hard to believe. Surely there had to have been other men in Deanna's life. A woman like her—she probably had to beat them off. But by the way she bit the corner of her lip and shook her head, he knew he was wrong.

She walked past him, close enough to smell her scent of vanilla mixed with the crispness of having spent the day outdoors, and he couldn't help himself. His hand shot out and captured hers. Deanna turned suddenly, no doubt shocked by the contact between them, which was laughable considering they'd been all over each other all day. But this was different, and they both knew it.

He rose to his feet and turned her gently so she faced him and let his fingers linger on her hip. "I'm glad I'll be your first."

HER HEART RACED SO HARD, she was sure he could hear it beat its frantic rhythm in her chest. From the moment she'd stepped out of the bathroom, there'd been a tension so thick in the room, she could hardly breathe. While she brushed her teeth, she'd tried to remind herself that it wasn't real. No matter how he'd kissed her, how her body had reacted to his touches, and how he looked at her, it was just a show. It wasn't real. *It wasn't real.*

But the way he looked at her at that moment felt pretty damn real.

"Marcus..." She shook her head. "I...we...I don't think—"

"I don't think we should think at all." He let his fingers

drop to the hem of her shirt where they danced over her bare thigh, teasing the edge.

"This can't happen."

"Why not?"

"Marcus, you know why not." She took a deep breath and turned away. She needed to put space between them because his proximity affected her thought process.

"I don't, actually." There was an edge in his voice so she turned to look at him. A muscle in his jaw twitched as he spoke. "Let's be honest, babe. I have no friggin' idea why this can't happen. And you know it."

They both knew what he wasn't saying, and as much as she never wanted to relive those days long ago when she'd run away from something that could have been real, she'd always known that embarking on this with him would bring up all those feelings again. It had just happened sooner than even she had expected.

"You want to talk?" Her question came out harsher than she'd intended, but it was too late to soften it. Besides, anger had always been a good defense mechanism. "Let's talk."

"It's about time." His hands clenched into fists at his sides, but she wasn't scared; he would never hurt her. It wasn't about that.

"What do you want to know?"

"Why did you leave?"

And there it was. His first question was the one she'd hoped to avoid. She shook her head and turned to look out the window at the dark mountain outside.

"No way." His hand wrapped around her shoulder and spun her around. "You don't get to do that." Deanna looked into his dark eyes, blazing with anger and passion. "You don't get to waltz back into town, blackmail me into playing this little game of yours and then dodge the one question I deserve an answer to. Hell no, Dee. I deserve an answer. I loved you."

His words sliced through her, but she stood strong and forced her body to hold her up.

"I can't explain it and I know it never should have happened." He laughed, but there was no humor in the sound. "Damn, we both know how fast it was. It's always been that way with us, hasn't it? Hard, fast, and so frickin' furious. Like a hurricane. I'm not even going to try to explain why, or how, but what I do know is that I fell for you and I think you felt it too." He held her arms in a grip she knew would leave bruises, but he wasn't hurting her. "Didn't you?"

She tried and failed to control her breathing. Her breasts rose and fell with hard, heaving breaths as she struggled to maintain a modicum of composure.

"Didn't you, Dee?" Marcus demanded. And then softer, he asked again, "Tell me you felt the same way, Dee. No matter what else happened, tell me that you loved me too."

His expression was so unguarded, so open and so real it cracked her in two. She didn't trust her voice to speak. Not really. She nodded and whispered, "I did." She looked directly in his eyes. "I loved you and it scared the hell out of me."

"You left."

"I couldn't stay. I could never stay in this town."

"Not for me."

"Not for anything."

"Dee." Marcus shook his head, but the heated anger was gone. "We could have made it work. We could have had it all." He released the grip on her arms and turned away to walk to the other side of the bed.

No. He couldn't do this to her: Tell her they could have had it all. Make her feel again. Ignite those old feelings that their day together had sparked and just turn away. "And now?" She spoke the question before she even knew she'd been thinking it. *What the hell did that even mean?* She didn't want anything with Marcus Stone now. Did she?

Casually, he stripped his shirt off and tossed it into the corner. The sight of his hard, naked chest only fueled her. She stalked over so she stood in front of him. He didn't answer her, but challenged her with his eyes.

"And now? It's just about the blackmail? Everything today? That was just pretending?"

She hated herself for opening herself up, but she couldn't help it. He'd ripped open the wound that was clearly still raw for both of them. And no matter the outcome, she was going to finish it.

He stepped closer, so they were so close she could feel the heat come off his naked chest. "I think you know the answer to that."

Dammit, she wanted—no, she needed—him to say it.

Instead, he reached up, plowed his fingers through her hair and pulled her head to his, catching her mouth in a hard, hungry kiss. She matched his intensity with her own need and raked her fingers down his hard, chiseled back. His hand holding her to him never let up but his free hand once again found the hem of her t-shirt, and pushed the fabric out of the way. His fingers went directly to her damp, hot core. He'd had her aroused all day and their fight had only intensified matters. Through the silky fabric, his fingers massaged her and drove her level of need even higher.

"You're so wet," he groaned into her mouth. "God, I want you."

The feeling was more than mutual. She fumbled with his belt and pulled it free before she yanked his jeans open. Her hands slipped inside his pants and released his hard, throbbing erection. But he didn't give her anytime to investigate her discovery because his hands gripped her hips and as if she weighed nothing, he lifted her.

Deanna wrapped her legs around him and brought her mouth to his again as he walked her backward. Instead of dropping her on the bed, he backed her into the wall with a force that shocked her. "Marcus, I—"

"Red," he growled. "I like."

Before she could respond, he tore her panties from her in one quick yank and held the scrap up before he stuffed them in his back pocket. "I'll buy you new ones." He kissed her hard and fast before he moved to her neck, where he nipped and nibbled, sucking her skin into his mouth in a move that would definitely leave a love bite behind. She didn't care. The only thing she cared about was the man who was working her into a frenzy.

"I need..." She tried to speak, but the words drifted off as his fingers once again returned to her core, this time with no fabric barrier.

"You need what exactly?" Marcus grinned and plunged a finger inside her. She moaned and arched her back, needing more. His thumb found her clit; he massaged and teased as he worked back and forth inside her until the sensations became too much. Deanna cried out her release, as she rode the wave higher and higher until she shattered around him, all the strength leaving her body.

THE WAY DEANNA unabashedly let herself go had almost been his undoing too. Marcus had to take more than a few deep breaths in order to pull himself together, but when she finally came to herself again and looked at him with those gorgeous, deep, dark eyes, her lids heavy with desire, it was more than lust that flowed through him, and it both pissed him off and worried him in equal measure.

"What?" she asked. Her face was flushed, her breaths still coming in hard, fast pants. "Is everything—"

"Damn, woman." It wasn't the most intellectual thing he

could say, but it was all he could think of as all the blood in his body had completely left his brain. He still held her pinned to the wall; his dick throbbed hard against her. "You are something else."

"I could say the same about you."

"Oh, you haven't seen nothing yet." He pulled back, securing his hands around her back, and took her to the bed, where he should have had her all along. He released her over the mattress, and she fell in a sinfully erotic heap on the mattress: her hair spread out behind her, her t-shirt hitched up, exposing her to him. The sight literally took his breath away. "Damn," he said again, wishing he could think of something even slightly smarter to say.

She moved to tug her t-shirt down, but he caught her hand in his. "No. I want to see you. You're beautiful."

Deanna's smile was so sweet, it tugged at his heart. He felt something he couldn't afford to feel.

That's not what this is about, he told himself. He needed to get back to basics. This was about sex. It wasn't about feeling anything. *Hell no.* Just sex. One night to get her out of his system. Then he could move on. Completely.

He reached into his back pocket and pulled out a condom before he shed his pants. "Take it off," he commanded and gestured to her shirt. She complied quickly and once she was completely naked, Marcus needed another moment to pull himself together. He'd waited almost three years to have her again; he wasn't going to blow it. He was going to enjoy every second of having Deanna Gordon beneath him again.

His hands skimmed her body, tracing lightly over her full breasts, taking in the dip of her waist and the swell of her hips. When he reached the top of her thighs, she quivered with the expectation of his touch, but he moved back up to focus on her nipples; he laved first one, and then the other with his tongue.

She arched her back and called out his name. He'd

forgotten that about her, how completely unaware or simply uncaring she was whether anyone heard her when they had sex. He tore open the foil packet and sheathed himself before he poised himself at her entrance. They locked eyes and there was no way he could look away or hold back. "Dee, I want you so much, you're...this..."

She nodded, as if she understood exactly what he was trying to say. Which she probably did. Because he could see it in her eyes. The knowledge that once they crossed that line again, there would be no going back. They would be setting themselves up for the same hurt and pain as before. But Marcus knew something she didn't. This time would be different, because he wouldn't let himself fall again. He held her gaze as he entered her, thrusting until he was fully seated inside her. *This time is different.* Her dark eyes widened, but she didn't close them. To watch her watching him was so intense, he knew he wouldn't be able to take much more. Deanna's fingers dug into his backside to urge him on and it was all the encouragement he needed.

They clung to each other, coming together seamlessly; their bodies responded to each other as if there had never been a distance between them. Soon he felt the telling tightening in her body just as he reached the point of no return. They'd always been in sync physically—it had been part of their connection then—and if anything, the time apart had only made it stronger. Together they crashed into their orgasms, Deanna crying out while he lost himself in her.

He didn't trust himself to speak for a few minutes. After being with her again, there was way too many things he wanted to say, but couldn't. *No.* He'd sworn to himself that he wouldn't lose himself to her again. He wouldn't let himself fall again. Not for her. But that was before his body had remembered what it was like to be inside her, to hold her, to—*no.*

He had to remain focused. He'd meant what he'd said to her earlier; they could have made it work. But that was then.

He wrapped his arms around her and pulled her into his body.

And now?

Her question echoed in his head and he kissed her bare shoulder. *And now?*

He had no idea.

Chapter Nine

SHE'D FALLEN asleep hard and fast and with Marcus's arm around her, slept soundly all night. But when she woke, and he was gone, Deanna couldn't help but replay the entire night in her mind. *What the hell?* What had she been thinking? The last thing she'd needed was to fall into bed with Marcus Stone. It couldn't happen. It shouldn't have happened. It certainly couldn't happen again. No matter how right it had felt to be with him again.

"Especially because of that." She pulled the cover over her head.

She'd never intended their little game to go so far. *But didn't you secretly hope it would?* She wasn't going to answer that question. Not even to herself. Hell no. Things had changed now; he'd changed. As much as she was glad Marcus wasn't there because she could definitely use the time to pull herself together, she knew he was nearby. This wasn't over. No. It was far from over.

But she couldn't put it off forever. Deanna flung the covers back and headed for the shower. If she was going to deal with

Marcus, she would at least need to wash the reminder of him from her body.

She took as long as possible in the shower and when she finally emerged, the smell of bacon and fresh coffee was enough to lure her downstairs and into the kitchen.

"Good morning." Malcolm was the first to greet her. He stood before the stove with a spatula in his hand and a smile that was so much like his brother's, who stood next to him, it was unsettling.

"Morning."

"Black, right?" Marcus walked around the kitchen island with a mug in his hand. "How did you sleep, babe?" He dropped a kiss on her forehead and brushed a strand of hair from her cheek with a touch so tender, she could almost forget it was all for show. Almost.

"Thank you." She took the mug from his hands and inhaled greedily. "I can't believe you remembered how I—" She broke off when she remembered they had an audience. "I slept great, because you were there." It was a sickly sweet thing to say, but it was also the truth. Having the heavy weight of his arm around her while she slept had been nice. Maybe even a little more than nice.

"You two are so damn cute." Deanna turned and laughed at Malcolm, who went back to tending the food on the stove. "I hope you're hungry."

"I'm starving." She gave Marcus a half smile and he returned to his station in the kitchen at the toaster. "It smells fantastic."

"You're getting the Stone special," Marcus said. "Nothing but the best for our women." He winked dramatically at her and she laughed. It was easy to fall into a comfortable rhythm with him. Maybe a little too easy. But it was fun, and why not enjoy it while she could? After all, just like everything else to do with the situation, it was temporary.

"Where is Kylie?"

"She had a little trouble sleeping last night."

"That's not good." Deanna took a sip of her coffee; the rush of caffeine filled her senses. "Was it the beers or the excitement of the day?"

"I think it had more to do with the noises coming from down the hall."

Deanna spun to see Kylie in the doorway. She looked exhausted, her hair piled into a messy ponytail, and her tired eyes stared directly at Deanna.

She blushed and a hand flew up to her mouth. "Oh." She glanced to Marcus, who was no help with a self-satisfied grin on his face, and then back to Kylie, who was clearly not impressed. "I'm so sorry, Kylie. I..." There was really nothing she could say without making the situation worse.

"Whatever." Kylie pulled out the chair next to Deanna at the eating bar and accepted the coffee Malcolm slid over to her. "It doesn't matter." Kylie wouldn't look at her and the rest of the breakfast was awkward, despite the yummy food and the effort both Marcus and Malcolm had put into it. Something was clearly going on with Kylie, and as much as she would have just liked to ignore it and move on, the tension was getting to be too much. When they finished eating, Deanna saw her opportunity to deal with it.

"Why don't you guys let us clear up?" she suggested.

"Yeah?"

"For sure," she insisted. "It's the least we could do. Right, Kylie?"

The other woman nodded, but still wouldn't meet her eyes. Deanna forced a smile. "Go into the other room. We got this. Really."

The men didn't need to be told twice. They disappeared without a backward glance to do whatever it was that men did on Sunday mornings, and Deanna gathered up the rest of the plates to take them to the sink.

"Men make such a mess when they cook, don't they?" She kept her voice light but Kylie wasn't having any of it.

She dropped a pile of plates in the sink with a crash, put her hand on her hip and spun so she faced Deanna, her eyes finally fixed on her. "So what's the deal?"

"Pardon?"

"You know what I'm talking about." Kylie's voice was laced with something that was dangerously close to resembling anger. "What's going on with you and Marcus?"

"We're dating." She forced a smile that likely looked as fake as it felt.

"No."

"Yes." Deanna assessed her old friend. What the hell did she mean, *no*? They were obviously dating. Well, not really. But to everyone else, they were. No matter what Kylie thought she knew, Deanna was definitely not about to confess a thing to her. Especially not when she was being such a bitch. "I'm not sure why you're questioning that."

"I'm not." Kylie shook her head. "But I am saying that there's something going on with you two. I just can't figure it out."

Deanna looked away. It would be a good time to confess their past history. She could come clean with Kylie right now. It would be easy and it might even make the whole situation better.

But it might not.

"I don't understand what you're implying." It would definitely be easier to play dumb. "There's nothing else going on."

Kylie turned her attention to the sink and squirted some soap in before she ran the water over the stack of plates. Deanna used the reprieve from Kylie's stare to take a deep breath and collect herself. "I'm sorry," Kylie said after a moment. "I'm not trying to be a bitch. I'm just tired."

"I really am sorry about last night."

Kylie glanced at her, a question in her eyes. "Everything with you and Marcus...it all happened really fast, don't you think? I mean, you haven't been back here that long and the way you two behave, it's as if you've known each other for years."

"Sometimes it's just like that, I guess." Deanna shrugged and took a clean, soapy plate out of Kylie's hands. "I can't explain it, really. But with some people, I guess there's just a really strong, instant connection." It definitely wasn't a lie. There was a strong connection between them. Always had been. "And we have known each other for years. We met when I was home for a break between med school and residency, remember?"

"I remember." Kylie spoke slowly, as though she was working through something in her head, which Deanna desperately hoped she wasn't. "That's when Marcus and I were —no." She gasped and the plate she'd been holding crashed into the sink with a splash.

She didn't want to, but there wasn't any choice. Deanna turned to look at Kylie, who shook her head, rage in her eyes. "You...and Marcus...no."

"Kylie. It wasn't like—"

"You were with him." She jabbed a soapy finger in Deanna's direction. "When I was dating him." It wasn't a question. It didn't need to be. "How could you—"

"Kylie." Deanna held up her hands, mostly because she thought Kylie might actually hit her. "It wasn't like that. I mean...it was, but—"

"You're my friend." She shook her head. "No. You were my friend."

The ground spun beneath her and the pancakes she'd just

eaten sat heavy in her stomach as Deanna tried to think of something, anything to say that would explain things to Kylie. The problem was, there was nothing she could say.

"You have nothing to say?"

"I—"

"Don't bother." She grabbed a towel and dried her hands before she threw it onto the counter. "I can't imagine that you'd have anything worthwhile to say." She turned to walk away and Deanna panicked.

"That's not fair," Deanna yelled after her. It was the wrong thing to do. Kylie spun on her heel. Rage filled her pretty face.

"Not fair? You think *I'm* not being fair? You slept with my boyfriend and lied to me."

That was the moment Malcolm and Marcus chose to return to the kitchen, no doubt drawn by the raised voices. They froze in the doorway, the expressions on their faces anything but identical. Malcolm's was lined with confusion and concern while Marcus had likely figured everything out. Although he looked slightly concerned, mostly he just looked as if he found the whole thing entertaining, which just pissed her off even more.

"You slept with me?" Malcolm shook his head and asked the ridiculous question.

Everyone ignored him and Deanna focused on Kylie again. She could not let a lifelong friendship end this way. Even though she knew she deserved Kylie's anger, she'd been a terrible friend and it was a guilt that had eaten at her for years. She had to try to fight to make things right. The knowledge that she was currently lying to her about her current relationship with Marcus wasn't lost on her, but there'd be time to deal with that later. She hoped. "Kylie," she tried again. "Please. Let's talk about this."

Kylie whirled around. "What exactly do you want to talk

about? The fact that you said you were my friend and lied to me or the fact that you whored yourself out to him?"

———

WHOA. That was too much for Marcus. The whole thing had been sort of entertaining for a split second, but the moment Kylie called Deanna a whore, that was too much. *Way* too much.

Marcus stepped into the room and put himself between the women. Not because he thought Kylie would hit Deanna or anything, but you never knew. He never would have expected Kylie to call Dee such hurtful things, either. And judging by the hurt look on Dee's face, she'd never expected it either.

"That's enough, Kylie."

Kylie's face twisted up. "Really? Coming from you, that's a pretty big statement."

"I thought we were good, Kylie?" And he did. Although he'd never really been sure how it was that Kylie had come to forgive him for being such a jerk while they were dating, she had. No doubt because she had no feelings whatsoever for him anymore.

"Past what?" Malcolm joined him. "What is going on here?"

"Marcus slept with Deanna," Kylie blurted.

Malcolm laughed, which judging by the pissed-off glare Kylie gave him, was not the right response. He cleared his throat. "Well, I think that's understandable, don't you? I mean, they're together." He waved between the two of them.

"No," Kylie said. "Before. When we were together. She slept with him while I was dating him."

Malcolm's face transformed and Marcus instantly felt guilty, protective, and pissed off all at once. Malcolm had always been in love with Kylie. From the moment they'd met her all those years ago, Malcolm had it bad. But Marcus pursued her. Largely because he could, and if it meant he'd win the girl, that's all that was important to him. Right from the start, he'd known it was wrong. She was with the wrong twin, and he'd regretted ever going after Kylie, especially because he'd seen the way his brother had pined for her. Marcus had never loved her, but he'd been a total and complete asshole by stringing her along and cheating on her instead of letting her go. He'd copped to it and apologized for it long ago, but it didn't mean all the old feelings couldn't be stirred up at a moment's notice.

Malcolm shook his head. "Unbelievable, man."

"Look." Marcus backed up so he stood next to Deanna. He slid his hand over hers and squeezed. "We didn't mean for it to happen."

"Her friend, Marcus?" He shook his head again, as if he simply couldn't believe what his brother had been capable of. "Even for you..."

"You have to believe me, Kylie," Deanna tried again. "I really didn't mean for it to happen. It killed me to lie to you." Marcus gave her hand another squeeze when she said that because he knew it was likely killing her to lie even as she apologized.

"Next you're going to tell me it was some sort of undeniable connection and that you tried, but you just couldn't...that is what you're going to say, isn't it?"

Marcus and Deanna both nodded, but it was Marcus who spoke. "Because it's true. I fell in love with her, Kylie." He felt Deanna stiffen next to him. "I'm so sorry. I was such a jerk to you back then, and you know I've changed. I've apologized, and I'll do it a million times if that's what it takes."

"I know, Marcus. And I...but with my *friend*?"

"We never meant to hurt you and we were going to tell you, but..." He didn't know how much he should say. Their situation was so damn complicated. But he had to remember, when they were done playing their little game, Deanna would be gone again and he'd be left to salvage some kind of relationship with his soon-to-be sister-in-law. But he had a goal of his own. And he knew the best way to achieve it. "She left me," he continued, making his decision. "I told her I loved her and wanted to tell you everything but Dee left, because she wanted to protect you. She chose your friendship over whatever she felt for me." Marcus could hear Deanna exhale next to him and he knew he'd won some points with her.

"Is that true?"

Deanna nodded. "Of course. I would always choose you. I never meant to be with him and it—"

"Did you love him, too?"

Silence filled the room. Marcus held his breath, suddenly needing to know the answer. All eyes were on Deanna.

"Yes." She spoke the word softly but Marcus heard it loud and clear.

"And now?"

Again, a question with an answer that would hold more weight than Kylie even knew. Marcus waited.

Deanna licked her lips and swallowed hard. She looked right at him, nothing but honesty in her eyes when she said, "Yes. I think I do."

Chapter Ten

DEANNA HAD DREADED GOING HOME and dealing with her parents and what would surely be some major judgment about Marcus, but as it turned out, by the time she got home after the party, her parents were gone for the day. Monday morning at breakfast, neither of them mentioned it at all. In fact, they seemed to go out of their way to avoid talking about the Slush Cup at all, which made for some very awkward conversations, but Deanna was still too emotionally drained from her confrontation with Kylie to get into it. The reprieve, however short it was sure to be, was welcome.

She was about to head out for work when her father stopped her. "Deanna." She turned. "Maybe we could grab some lunch today?" her father asked. "I'd like to go over a few things with you."

So much for a reprieve.

"I'd love to, Dad. But I promised Sam I'd meet up with her to help her make plans for Beth's bridal shower. Did you hear the news?" She looked at her mother when she asked the question, but her mom steadfastly avoided making eye contact.

"Beth and Slade set a date." Still, no reaction. She looked back to her father.

"We heard," he said.

"And?"

"It's great news."

"Of course it is." Deanna shook her head. Her parents were impossible to figure out. "And it's all going to happen so fast. I can't imagine planning a wedding so quickly, but I guess they have people who—"

"Can you imagine planning a wedding at all?"

Deanna turned to stare at her mother, who looked as if she was about to burst into tears. *The silent treatment sure didn't last long.* "Pardon me? No." She looked quickly between both her parents, but her dad just shook his head. "Why would I be planning a wedding? I'm not—ohh." All at once it became clear. "You think I'm going to marry Marcus?"

"No, of course—"

"You said you were—"

They spoke at once. Gayle bit down on her knuckle and looked away, so it was her father who picked up the conversation. "It's not that we think you're going to get married to Marcus, Deanna. It's just that you did say you were serious and—"

"How could you be serious with him so quickly?" Her mother jumped up from the table, but then sank back into her chair as if she didn't have the strength to stand. "You've only just got back and we always thought you would..."

"I would what?"

Gayle shook her head and wouldn't look at Deanna. She'd known this conversation would be coming—she certainly didn't think it would happen so quickly after announcing their fake relationship—but maybe she'd underestimated her parents' desire to see her settled down with a *good boy* and more than that, she'd likely underestimated her parents' dislike for

Marcus Stone. Everything seemed to be working according to her twisted little plan, but somehow instead of feeling satisfied, something else was going on inside her. And it felt an awful lot like discontent.

"What did you think, Mom?"

"We thought you would choose someone different for your mate." Her father answered.

It was easy to see the effort the conversation was costing her dad, but Deanna knew she had to stay committed. *Might as well go in for the kill.* "Well, it is a small town." She nodded and tried to look casual. "And there really aren't a lot of single men in town. Besides, you said yourself that I'm getting older and if I wanted to settle down, I should start looking."

"We didn't mean you had to look right away."

Deanna was fairly positive her mother was about to start crying, and as guilty as it made her feel, she tried to stay focused. Ultimately, her mother would be happier if she was back in Toronto, married to the type of guy she'd always wanted for Deanna. *But what if that's no longer what you want?* The little voice in the back of her head piped up. It was a really inconvenient time to start thinking along those lines, so she pushed it down.

"Mom. It's fine." Deanna gathered up her things again. "Dad, can we maybe talk about whatever it is you need to talk about this afternoon? I only have patients in the morning. So whenever you're free, just let Karen know, okay?"

Her dad nodded and smiled. She was just about out the door when he grabbed her arm and she turned once more. "It really is nice having you at the practice, Deanna. I'm really proud of you and how well you've taken to the patients."

"Dad..."

"It's no big deal." He waved his hand in front of his face and smiled sadly. "But it's been really nice working with you. I just wanted you to know."

Something inside her threatened to crack if she didn't get out of there and get some air. But before she did, Deanna leaned forward and kissed her dad on the cheek. "I think so, too, Dad." Then, before she let them see the unshed tears in her own eyes, she turned and disappeared out the door.

She sucked in a breath of fresh air and exhaled slowly. Things were getting complicated. Too complicated.

MARCUS MOVED his pencil quickly across the page, sketching out his latest design for a board. What had started out as a hobby while he was out on the circuit had started to become more than that. The ideas kept coming into his head and more than ever, he wanted to see them produced and not just as sketches in his notebook. Maybe he'd have more time coming up to look into getting some prototypes done up. He had some money saved up and now that the hill was officially closed for the season, things were definitely going to slow down for him. He knew he was going to have to figure things out soon. The fact was, during the summer months, there wouldn't be much for him to do at Stone Summit, if anything. Which meant getting back on the circuit was looking better and better. Not that he'd be boarding through the summer, but the season ran longer in Europe and if he took the movie deal, that would mean work right away.

But that was a big *if*.

First, he'd need the results from his drug test. Not that he was worried about them. There was no doubt he was clean. What he was worried about was Deanna. Things had gone further than he'd expected the other night and as much as he'd been aching to get her in his bed again, he hadn't really intended to. Well, not so fast anyway. But that's just how things were with the two of them. Fast and intense.

But what really worried him was what she'd said in the kitchen the next day when things had gotten heated with Kylie. Did she really love him? Already? Sure, that was his intention: make her fall and then leave. She was going to hurt the way he'd been hurt. But he hadn't really expected her to fall in love with him. Not so fast anyway. *No.* There was no way she really meant what she'd said. It was all part of the show; chances were good that he'd never be able to make her fall for him again and the whole charade would end. They'd both go on with their lives and he'd never get his retribution.

Marcus dropped his head in his hands and groaned. Part of him wanted that: wanted to get even, to make her hurt. But there was another, possibly growing, part of him that wanted to protect her from any hurt at all, let alone be the source of that pain.

"Dammit." He struck his fist on the table. It was happening again. Something about the woman got under his skin and made him want things he had no business wanting. Especially not with her.

"What's up, brother? Rough night?"

Marcus popped his head up. Malcolm walked through the kitchen, poured himself a cup of coffee and lounged against the counter. Kylie had flown back to Vancouver the day before, shortly after the big scene in the kitchen. And even though everyone had made up and expressed their apologies, he wasn't dumb enough to know it would be over so quickly.

"I'm just thinking about things." Marcus scrubbed a hand through his hair and held his own mug out for a refill, to which Malcolm complied.

"That's dangerous." His brother laughed. "Don't hurt yourself."

"Funny guy." He took a sip of his coffee. Maybe more caffeine would give him clarity. "You look awfully chipper for a guy whose fiancée is gone and whose business is closed. Shouldn't you be crying into your pillow or something?"

"Hey." Malcolm shrugged. "It was a great first season. Nothing to be upset about there. Besides, spring happens. It's not like I can stop the seasons from turning. Besides, I'm tossing around some ideas to open up a mountain biking center during the summer months."

Marcus nodded. It was a good idea and one a lot of ski hills were turning to for the summers.

"And as far as sending Kylie back to school." Malcolm drank some more coffee before he set his mug down. "I hate it, of course, but she needs to go do her thing, and that's cool. Besides, it'll give you some time to figure out what the hell you're doing with Deanna. And, maybe you could get that sorted out before Kylie gets back. Because as much as I love starting my mornings with female drama, I can imagine it would get old—quick."

"Yeah, about that—"

"Hey." Malcolm held up his hand. "I don't need to know the details. Just let me know when it's all done." He turned away and opened the fridge.

Marcus could have let it go at that, and done what his brother had suggested and *deal with it*, but something about Malcolm's choice of words bothered him. A lot.

"Done?"

Malcolm rummaged through the fridge and pulled out a jug of milk. "What?"

"Done?" Marcus repeated. "You said to let you know when it was all done." Marcus leaned back in his chair. "What did you mean by that?"

Malcolm shrugged and moved around his kitchen as if he was totally unaware of the storm that brewed within his brother. Which he likely was. "Just that," he said. "Let me know when whatever is happening between the two of you is over so I can let Kylie know and she can chill."

"What makes you think it's going to be over?" He wasn't trying to argue or be antagonistic, but despite the fact that Marcus himself knew it would be over because it wasn't really anything to begin with, he couldn't help it. He was pissed at the idea that his brother would just assume that his relationship would end.

Malcolm must have heard something in his voice because he put his bowl down and looked at Marcus again. "Come on," he said. "Of course it's going to end."

"Why should it?" He clenched his fingers into a fist under the table and spread them again slowly.

"Marcus. Really?" Malcolm crossed his arms over his chest. "Do we really have to do this?"

"Apparently we do because I don't understand what the hell you're implying."

"You and Deanna," he started. "You'll never last and you and I both know it. It's just a fling."

But it wasn't. It was so much more than a fling and as much as he hated it, Marcus knew it. Deanna had always been more than just some piece of ass. Even with the crazy situation they were in, it was still more. He tilted his head and tensed his jaw, but didn't say anything, so Malcolm continued.

"She's a doctor, for God's sake, and you're—"

"I'm what?" Marcus shoved his chair backward and stood. "A snowboarder? A loser? A screw-up? Is that what you were going to say?"

"No. Come on, Marc, that's not what I was going to say. What's going on with you?"

He couldn't answer that question, because the problem was, all of those things he'd just said—they were true. It was exactly why things were going to end with Deanna, real or not; she'd blackmailed him into being her fake boyfriend. Even if what he'd felt for her was real. And even if she'd meant what she'd said, and she did love him. It would never work.

He slammed his fist on the table. Coffee splashed everywhere.

"What the hell is wrong with you, Marcus?"

Another question he couldn't answer properly. "Every-thing," he growled instead and shoved the chair. It crashed to the floor; he stormed out of the kitchen and out of the house.

"SO YOU'LL HELP ME?" Samantha asked her for at least the third time.

Deanna smiled and put her fork down. She spent the majority of their lunch date convincing Sam that she would in fact help her throw Beth a bridal shower that weekend. She had managed to get a few bites of her club sandwich in, but she couldn't help but notice that Sam had barely touched her salad at all. "You know I'll help you," Deanna said. "But I do think we should keep it simple. I'm sure Beth will appreciate anything as long as her friends are there. You don't have to go crazy."

"I know, I know." Sam stabbed a few pieces of lettuce but instead of putting them in her mouth, she waved her fork. "But she's my best friend, you know, and she was so amazing with my wedding I just want to do everything I can for her."

"I'm sure Beth knows that." Deanna tried to sound as reas-suring as possible. The fact that she didn't have a best friend of her own was only a minor detail, but she could imagine that Beth knew how much Sam cared about her. "I'm also sure that Beth knows how busy you are and doesn't expect you to drop everything because of her last-minute wedding."

Samantha stared at her as if she'd lost her mind. She shook her head and picked at her salad some more.

"What I meant was...never mind. Let's go over the details again." Deanna flipped the pages of the notebook where she'd taken a few notes of things they'd do. "You said Trent was going to arrange the private room at the Stillwater restaurant?"

Sam nodded.

"Great. So maybe if the chef can prepare some light appetizers and some punch, that should be adequate for food and drinks. I'll get Cynthia to help me order some flowers from Petal Pushers for the tables and we'll keep it really simple and pretty. Do you have a list of people we should invite? It's been so long since I've been here, I wouldn't really know where to begin."

"Everyone loves Beth," Sam said. "You could pretty much invite everyone in town and that would work."

Deanna gave her a look. There was no way she was going to invite everyone in town. They were trying to keep it simple. Besides, as far as she knew, they were still supposed to be keeping the details of the wedding under wraps.

"Okay," Sam relented. "I'll do the invitations."

"Perfect." Deanna closed her notebook. "Then I think that's it." She didn't mention that she planned on booking Beth and Sam some spa treatments to enjoy together. They needed some relaxation time together and there was no doubt they both deserved a little break.

"Thank you so much, Dee. I can't even tell you how thankful I am for all your help. Things have been so crazy."

Deanna picked at the crust of her sandwich, letting the bread flake onto her plate. "So you haven't had much chance to hire anyone yet?" What she really wanted to ask was whether she'd had time to relax and spend time with Trent. But she wasn't there as a doctor, so if Sam wanted to talk about making babies, she'd let her bring it up on her own.

"Well, I did get some help lined up for the summer." Sam smiled. "Jess is going to start right away. She needed a little break from health care after Cynthia's mom passed and wanted something fun for the summer. The other new hire won't be here until June. But I suppose things will calm down a little now until the summer season starts. With the skiers gone, it shouldn't be quite as crazy."

"That's true. So who else did you hire?"

Sam shook and took a sip of her drink. "You'll never guess."

"Then tell me." Deanna laughed.

"Do you remember the McCormicks?"

Deanna racked her brain. From the moment she'd set foot back in Cedar Springs, people had asked her if she remembered their brother, or a cousin, or some long-lost teacher that they'd had in third grade. Some she actually remembered; most she didn't. But Sam looked at her with so much expectation, she almost hated to let her down.

"Think back to summers on the lake," Sam prodded. "Bonfires and—"

"No?" Deanna gasped and her hand flew to her mouth. "The McCormicks? As in, the summer people McCormicks?"

Sam nodded and laughed.

Growing up in Cedar Springs, summer had always been their favorite time of year because it meant long days on the lake: swimming, water-skiing if someone could get their hands on a boat, and floating on rafts, sipping contraband beer. The nights were just as long and hot with bonfires on the beach and campouts in the trees. The summer was always made just a little more interesting with the arrival of the *summer people*, who came at the end of June and took up residence in the big log cabins just outside of town, along the lakefront. They stayed until Labor Day weekend. And for Deanna, Samantha, and the rest of the Cedar Springs girls, their arrival also meant the opportunity for teenage summer romances. The McCormicks were one of those families. With four boys—four *good-looking* boys, who all had big allowances—they were usually high in demand.

"Wow." Deanna laughed. "I haven't thought about them in years." And she hadn't, even though it had been Ian McCormick, the oldest, who'd been her briefly lived seasonal boyfriend the summer before her senior year. They'd had a lot of fun together, and she'd lost her virginity to him—memories that never failed to bring a smile to her face. She smiled now, just thinking about him.

"I know. Neither had I. There hasn't been anyone in that house in years. In fact, a lot of those old summer places have been empty for a while. I guess Cedar Springs was just too far to go, or wasn't as glamorous as some of the other resort towns."

Sam spoke casually, but Deanna could hear the resentment behind her words. Cedar Springs had gone through some tough times. Being a little farther from the major cities than other lake towns, people stopped visiting for a while and those other towns built up their businesses, while those in Cedar Springs had struggled. Including the Grizzly Paw. It wasn't until recently that things had picked up again.

"I guess things are changing around here again."

"They are," Sam agreed. "And more and more of the summer families are starting to come back."

"Including the McCormicks."

Sam nodded.

"So are they going to work for you? Those boys must be our age, and don't take this the wrong way, but why would they want to work here?" Deanna knew Sam wouldn't be offended. It wasn't about working at the Paw; it was just that the summer people never seemed to work at all. They just had an endless supply of money.

"It's not really them," Sam said. "Well, at least it's not the brothers themselves, but their kids or cousins or something. I'm honestly not really sure what the connection is. But I got an email from Ian McCormick mentioning that he'd be arriving for the summer with a young woman who was looking for a job. All I know is she's twenty-one and needs a job."

"That's all you know?"

Sam shrugged. "Look, I was desperate and if it doesn't work out, I can always let her go."

"True. But who is she?" Deanna could barely even believe what she was saying. She'd easily fallen back into the small-town gossip circle. Maybe too easily. All she knew was that if everyone in town was going to be gossiping about the McCormicks, it meant they weren't going to be gossiping about her and Marcus, and that was definitely fine with Deanna. Especially when their situation was getting a little too complicated.

"It doesn't even matter to me." Sam laughed. "I'm telling you, I just need a little help. Especially since I have this great idea for Archer."

"What's that?"

"It's kind of crazy," Sam started. "Especially right now when the Paw is so busy. I mean, I shouldn't even be thinking about such a thing, but—"

"What?"

Sam looked around to make sure they weren't being over-heard. "Archer's birthday is coming up and I'm going to get everyone to chip in for a plane ticket."

"What? Where?"

Sam laughed. "I don't know yet. That's the best part."

"Does he even want to go anywhere?" Archer had always struck Deanna as the type of guy who would live and die in Cedar Springs. He loved everything about mountain life. She never thought of him as the traveling type.

"I don't know." Sam shrugged and pushed away her mostly untouched salad. "But I think he should. I love Archer dearly, but he's kind of spinning his wheels here. I mean, he needs to find someone and fall in love. But sometimes, you need to get out and see the world."

"You sound like that's what you'd like." Deanna winked at her. "Are you sure you're not projecting?"

"Of course I'd like that, too. But I think it would be good for him to go do some traveling. I'm thinking if everyone chips in fifty dollars, we could get him a backpack and a ticket to Central America or something."

Deanna shook her head and laughed. "You know I'll chip in. You're a good friend. Even if Archer won't know what hit him." Right then, her phone vibrated in her pocket. She fished it out to see a text from Marcus.

WHERE ARE YOU? *Call me?*

"SORRY," she said to Sam. "It's Marcus. I need to…"

"No problem." Sam winked at her. "We're going to talk about that situation, too," she added. "Don't think we aren't." Deanna opened her mouth to say something, but Sam just laughed. "Go, take care of your man. Thanks for everything. Lunch is on me."

Deanna gave her friend a quick hug and slipped outside into the sunshine, where she dialed Marcus's number.

"Where are you?"

"Well, hello to you too." Deanna smiled and looked out toward the lake. It was such a beautiful spring day, she'd be happy to play hooky for the afternoon and go for a walk to look for crocuses and pussy willows. "I'm just down by the lake." She left the sidewalk behind to pick her way along the beach. "It's beautiful out here. I was thinking—"

"I need my test results."

His demand took her off guard and she stumbled. She'd forgotten all about the results of the drug test. In fact, for a moment she'd forgotten all about the fact that they weren't actually dating. Not really. The truth hit her like a blow.

"Deanna? Are you still there?"

She took a deep breath and straightened her jacket, even though he couldn't see it. "Right." She hoped she sounded more put together than she felt. "Your results. I'll check on them this afternoon."

"Good." His voice was curt and clipped, as if he were agitated by something. Or someone.

"They might not be ready yet," she added. The sudden need to cry overwhelmed her, and she hated herself for it. She wasn't Marcus's girlfriend; she needed to remember that. If he was rude or short with her, it didn't matter. They weren't a couple. That had been her choice. "Sometimes they take a few days. Sometimes longer if the lab is backed up."

"That's fine," he said. "And thank you." There was the sound of a throat clearing on the other end of the line and then he added, "Maybe I could take you out later this week?"

Her heart soared, which was ridiculous. "Sure." She hoped it sounded calm and indifferent.

"Wednesday?" he asked. "Will your parents be home?"

Why would he need to know that? Was he hoping for another hookup? Likely. But that was a one-time, scratch-an-itch type of thing. And regardless of what she may have said afterwards, it wasn't about anything more than sex. It couldn't happen again. No matter how much she might want it to. No. *Especially* because of how much she wanted it to. "Why would that matter?"

Marcus chuckled. "Because convincing your parents that we're in love works better when they can see it."

Right. "Yes, they should be home."

"Great. I'll pick you up at eight."

She hung up the phone and stared at the calm lake before her. Suddenly, playing hooky and going for a walk didn't seem nearly as appealing as it had a few minutes ago. They were playing a game. That was it. She needed to get control of the situation. And fast. The sooner her parents saw things her way, the sooner she could get out of town, and away from the feelings that were threatening to become a little too real.

Chapter Eleven

MARCUS DIDN'T EXPECT to get his test results until his date, or whatever it was, with Deanna, but to his surprise, she had them sent over to his house in a sealed enveloped the next day. He'd ripped them open to check the results, not that he was worried, but he hadn't been worried the first time and look how that turned out. Of course they were clean and after a quick call to his coach, he scanned them in and sent the email that would get him back on the circuit. Just like that, he'd be back in the snowboarding world and away from Cedar Springs. And Deanna.

The fact that she'd held up her end of their deal before her goal had been accomplished wasn't lost on Marcus. Things had shifted between them; it felt different. More real. If that was even possible. Things always felt so bloody real with Deanna— that was the problem. But for the next few days before his date with her, it was all he could think of. She'd said she was falling for him again. She stood there in his kitchen and told Kylie that, but he knew it was meant for him and he couldn't get the look on her face out of his mind.

But it wasn't real and he needed to keep reminding

himself of that. Whatever was happening between them, it was all an act. But he'd said he would take her out, and he would.

He just needed to keep his feelings out of it.

It was a tiny, yet important detail that he ignored as he got out of the shower Wednesday evening and selected his clothes. He'd decided to keep his date with Deanna low-key. If it was a real date, he would have planned something much different, and much more private. But the goal was to be seen, so he'd make damn sure they would be. At least as much as they could be on a Wednesday night.

"Okay, I'm out of here, Koda." He scratched the puppy behind his ears and the dog licked his hand in response. He'd have to talk to Malcolm about letting Koda stay with him while he went back on the circuit. It was exactly what everyone had been worried about when he took the dog, but his head was in a different place then. He'd actually planned to stay. Plans changed. "I'll be back later, buddy."

He swallowed down the guilt as he slid out the front door, avoiding his brother as well, the way he'd been doing for the last few days. He didn't even recognize the man he was becoming with all the lies and sneaking around. Sure, he'd had his share of misdeeds when he was younger, but he'd changed since then and now, all because of a woman, he was turning into someone he didn't even recognize.

Not just any woman. Deanna.

He used the time driving down the mountain into town to pull himself together. Deanna had held up her side of the bargain and delivered the test results. There was still a chance she could let it slip about the test, but somehow he knew she wouldn't. He could walk into her house and end their entire deception by telling Doctor Gordon and his wife the truth, right now, tonight. He could end the torture he was going through and be honest with everyone. And then he could pack his bags, get back on the circuit and leave Cedar Springs and Deanna Gordon behind once and for all.

The streetlights were just starting to come on when he pulled up in front of Deanna's house. He slammed the door of his truck, headed up the walk and rang the bell, still undecided about how he was going to play the situation. He hoped it would come to him when he saw her, but when the door opened and he saw Deanna looking delicious in a skirt that hit just above her knees to showcase her amazing legs and a simple blouse unbuttoned just enough that he could make out the swell of her breasts, all the blood drained from his head and the decision-making process got decidedly harder.

"Hi." Her smile lit up her face.

"Hi yourself."

"Come in." She stepped back and waved him inside. "Just let me grab my coat."

He took a step inside and stuffed his hands in his back pocket. "Deanna?" Marcus turned at the sound of Dr. Gordon's voice. "Who's at the—oh."

Marcus held his hand out. "Good evening, Dr. Gordon."

The man looked at his hand and looked away. "I assume you're here for Deanna?"

"She's just getting her coat."

"And where are you going?"

This was his moment. He had a choice to make. He could end it all right now, or—

"Dad." Deanna returned and put her hand on her father's arm. She looked over to Marcus with so much trust in her eyes that Marcus knew he couldn't betray it. At least not like that. "Leave Marcus alone. He's here to take me out on a nice date." Deanna leaned over to give him what he knew would be a chaste kiss on the cheek. But he wasn't having it.

No way.

If he was playing this game, he was all in.

Before she could react, Marcus wrapped an arm around her and turned her so she was firmly in his grasp as he dipped her low, dramatically and totally cliché, before he kissed her thoroughly. It was not something he'd ever normally do in front of a girl's father, but there was nothing normal about their situation.

The sound of a throat clearing broke through his consciousness and just in time, too, because it was way too easy to get lost in kissing Deanna.

He stood and lifted Deanna, giving her a chance to straighten her blouse before he turned to look at her father, who looked far from pleased. They stood in uncomfortable silence for a few moments before Deanna grabbed Marcus's hand and tugged him to the door. "We should get going. We're going to be late for...well, for whatever it is we're doing."

IT FELT OFF. Everything between them felt off. The second they got into the truck, it was all wrong. Not that it ever felt right, but even after that kiss—no, *especially* after that kiss—as she sat next to Marcus in his truck, the distance between them felt much wider than just the bench seat. The problem was, Deanna didn't know how it was supposed to feel. Only a few days ago, she thought she might actually be falling in love with him. Which was totally crazy, because it wasn't real. Nothing about the situation was real. Except it had been real. The way she'd felt with his hands all over her body, his mouth on hers. All of it. It felt real. It felt like it used to feel. And she needed to keep reminding herself what the situation really was.

"You got your test results?" she blurted, needing to fill the silence.

Marcus nodded. "I did. Thanks."

"I was going to wait until tonight to give them to you but I thought you might need them, and—"

"Thank you, Deanna." He nodded again, but didn't take his eyes off the road.

What the hell? What had shifted? Why was he so detached? She wasn't the type of woman to sit back and wonder.

"Where are we going?"

"The Paw." He shrugged. "There aren't a lot of choices and I figured you'd want to be as public as possible."

She nodded, because it was true. But what she really wanted to do was ask him what the hell was going on with him and why all of a sudden she was getting the cold shoulder. She wanted to ask him all kinds of things, but she didn't, because they pulled up in front of the Paw and Marcus hopped out before she had the chance. He came around the truck, opened her door and offered his hand. The second she stood next to him, he wrapped his arm around her and led her inside.

The shift in him was immediate. His hand slipped down, so it rested dangerously close to her breast, and before they could even find an open table, he'd pulled her in for a short, but very sexy kiss. He was playing his role. And he played it too damn well.

They walked through the room, which was surprisingly busy for a Wednesday night, and Marcus waved and called out to people he knew until all eyes were on them. "Should we grab a drink or would you rather dance and show them all how it's really done?" Without waiting for an answer, he spun her around and pulled her in tight to him, and although her body thrilled at his touch and the hard length of him pressed up against her, there was another feeling too.

Anger. Whatever was going on with him, she didn't need or want to be part of it.

Marcus swayed her to the beat of some country song she'd

been hearing all over the radio, but she locked her feet to the ground and refused to move.

"What's wrong?" He bent and nibbled her neck, but Deanna squirmed away, forcing him to look up.

"Take me home," she said through gritted teeth.

"Pardon?"

"Take. Me. Home."

To his credit, Marcus stepped back, took her hand and led her out the door. As soon as they were in the fresh air, Deanna shook free from his grasp.

"What the hell, Dee?"

Really? She needed a moment before she even attempted to answer him. She took a deep breath in and exhaled slowly before she decided it wasn't worth it. He knew exactly what was wrong. He wasn't stupid, and even if she hated it, Marcus knew her too well. "I'm not doing this."

"Yes," he said. "You are."

"Fine." He wanted to do this—she'd do it. "I'm not going to be your entertainment." She crossed her arms over her chest, mostly to keep her from shaking, she was so mad. "What was that in there?"

"That was dating." He sneered at her, and she had to fight the urge to smack him. "Isn't that what you wanted? For everyone to think we're together?"

She exhaled slowly. *When did he turn into such an asshole?* Just the other day, she'd actually enjoyed spending time with him. This Marcus was different. She didn't like it. Not at all.

No. She wasn't going to do this. Not with him. Not like this. She shook her head, turned away and started to walk.

"Deanna?"

She ignored him. It was a small town. It wouldn't take too long to walk home. She ignored the pinching in her feet and picked up the pace. She definitely hadn't chosen her shoes for their comfort, and had she thought for a moment she'd be walking, she wouldn't have given a second thought about how hot her legs looked in them.

"Where are you going?"

"Home." He was right behind her but she didn't turn around.

"You can't go home. Your parents will know—"

"I don't care." She stopped so suddenly he almost ran into her. "Let them think we had a fight. Let them know the truth. I don't care. But I'm not doing that anymore."

His eyes flared with his temper. "Do what exactly?"

She pressed her lips together.

"You mean do exactly what you asked me to do?" He laughed but there was no humor in it. "That's all I'm doing, Deanna. Exactly what you asked me to. No, wait. What you *blackmailed* me to do."

Heat rushed through her; she stood tall and glared at him. "You weren't complaining the other night." She'd be dammed if she was going to stand here and let him put all of this on her. Yes, she'd instigated their whole situation. It was a mess and it had been stupid and...it didn't matter. Because he'd played along. Really well. Maybe too well. "In fact," she pushed, "you seemed to think it was a pretty freaking good idea."

Deanna needed to get out of there. She refused to let him see the way he affected her. She turned again, determined this time to get away. It didn't matter whether her feet were blistered and bruised by the time she got home—she was not sticking around.

"Deanna!"

She didn't look back, but picked up her pace.

He yelled again, but she still didn't look back. She heard the footsteps behind her seconds before Marcus's hand grabbed her arm and spun her around. "Enough."

Anger flared through her, and she tried to jerk her arm away but he held her fast. "Let. Me. Go."

"I will not." He relaxed his grip a little, but not enough for her to get away. "Not until you tell me what is going on with you."

She shook her head and tried to look away but the intensity in his eyes held her. "I don't want to do this anymore." She managed to get the words out. She wasn't even sure it was true. If she gave up their deception, it would make it harder to leave. But not impossible. She'd never actually needed Marcus to get what she wanted and she knew it. "It's over," she said, resolved in her decision. "You don't have to—"

His lips on hers, crushing her into a heated kiss, swallowed the rest of her words. His free hand came to her face and held her tight, but his other hand never released her arm. "It's far from over," he growled against her mouth.

IF SHE THOUGHT she was going to end things so easily, she didn't have a clue about how things were really going to go down. She also didn't have any idea of the effect she had on him. Of course, up until a few minutes ago, Marcus hadn't even been sure of it himself. But seeing her so angry and heated because of him, and then watching her walk away...no. It wasn't happening. She'd gotten under his skin and it was a bad idea, certainly. There was nothing good that could come out of it, but he'd be damned if he could help himself.

She opened her mouth to say something, but he kissed her again; this time he released her arm so he could twist both of his hands through her hair. Her mouth opened to him and he took it greedily. Marcus didn't want to want her so bad. To need her with his very being. Kissing her was the last thing he should be doing because now that he'd had a taste of her again, he wasn't going to want to let her go and that's exactly what he needed to do. What he should have done when he'd gone to pick her up.

He'd gotten what he needed from her and everything else had just been a distraction he didn't need. Which was why he should have just walked away. He should have let her go and ended the little game they had going with her parents. He could turn around and walk away, grab his snowboard and go. But he couldn't. The woman pulled him to her.

A low grown escaped her lips and the sound hit Marcus right in the gut. A feeling that quickly shot down to his groin, where he reacted hard and fast.

Not caring if they stood on Main Street, exposed to the entire town, Marcus pulled the back of her head closer to him, until her entire body with all its delicious curves was pressed right up against him. It was his turn to groan when her body met his and he could feel the heat of her through their layers of clothing. He wanted her, badly, and the fire was set to consume him if he didn't extinguish the flames soon.

He backed her up, moving her until they were pressed up against the side wall of the bakery Dream Puffs, just out of sight from anyone who happened to be passing by. Even if someone looked in their direction, Marcus knew they'd be hidden from view. And if they weren't...he didn't care.

"I...oh..." She tried to form a thought, but like him, there was obviously no room for thinking.

"I need you, Dee." That was the biggest understatement he could have thought of, but he couldn't think of much more. He pulled back from her delicious mouth, just long enough to issue a warning. "Say the word and I'll stop." He kissed her again, sucking her lower lip into her mouth briefly before he added, "But just know...that's the last thing I want."

She moaned again as his hand found her breast and squeezed and teased it through the fabric of her top. "I don't..."

He froze, her nipple between his fingers. If she told him to stop, he would. There was no doubt. But every fiber in his body wanted and needed for him to keep going. This woman...she belonged with him. Even if for only one more night.

But he wouldn't think of that now. No. Nothing but this: Deanna in front of him, the taste of her on his lips, the—

"I don't want you to stop." Her words came out as puffs of air.

It was all he needed to hear. His hand plunged down the v-neck of her top and slipped under the fabric of her bra to cup her full, luscious breast. He bent; his mouth latched over the hard bud he'd exposed. He sucked just enough to elicit another moan from her. The sound was almost enough to make him come completely undone.

Her hands slipped up his sides, under the fabric of his shirt; her head tipped back against the brick wall as she gave in to the sensations he knew he was creating in her.

There were a million reasons he should walk away right now before it could go any further. This woman had been nothing but trouble for him. She was the only woman who'd ever broken his heart. But she'd also been the only woman who could make him feel the way he was feeling. And even if it was only one more time, he needed her. Badly.

Deanna was obviously thinking the same way because her hands slipped down his chest to the buckle of his belt. He let out a long breath as she slipped the leather free and pulled his zipper down.

"You're going to be the death of me," he growled before his mouth found hers again.

"Good." With her hands wrapped around his length, he pulsed in her grip. Her grin was wicked and she freed him from the confines of his jeans.

Marcus could no longer hold himself back. He hitched up

her skirt and ran his fingers along the skimpy lace panties he found. "I hope you're not very attached to these." He hooked a finger under the elastic.

"Why is—"

With a firm tug, he tore the delicate panties away and the question died on her lips. Without giving her even a moment to process, his fingers found her heat, and pressed on her clit. She reacted strong and fast; her whole body quaked with need. A need his own body mirrored. He needed to be inside her. With his hands on her hips, he lifted her and her legs came around him. He poised to enter her and froze. "Dee, I don't have a—"

"It's okay. I'm protected."

"But, I—"

"Marcus." Even in the dim light, he could see the seriousness and heat in her eyes. "I trust you."

It was all he needed to hear. Hell, it was more than he needed to hear. There was so much meaning in those three little words. But he couldn't focus on what they meant beyond that exact moment. He shifted his hips and with his eyes locked on hers, slid into her tight, welcoming heat.

Chapter Twelve

DEANNA WAS STILL PROCESSING what had happened with Marcus when he dropped her off. She was so completely satisfied, yet totally confused at the same time. What was it about the man that caused her to be full of rage one minute and then blinded by lust the next? The emotions and sensations he evoked in her were too intense; she wasn't sure how to process everything that had happened and everything she felt.

But when she walked through her front door and saw the light was still on in the living room, she knew there was one thing she did have to do. Things had gone on long enough.

"Dad?" Deanna paused in the doorway and waited to see whether her dad was asleep in his chair or actually reading the paper he held. She knew he'd been waiting up for her, and guilt flashed through her knowing she'd caused him to miss out on sleep because of her actions. "Are you awake?"

He turned in the chair. His face looked tired and older than it should have. "How was your evening?"

She ignored the question, because there was no way she could answer it. She moved across the room and settled onto the ottoman across from his chair. "You didn't have to wait up."

He nodded and rubbed a hand over his face. "Of course I did, Dee. You're my baby girl. I'll always worry about you. Besides, we needed a chance to talk and there just hasn't been time lately."

"I know. I'm sorry."

"No." He shook his head sadly. "I'm sorry. I know asking you to come here and help me out at the practice wasn't fair. I never should have put you in that position. You have a life in Toronto, and as much as I wish your life was here, I have to accept that. You can't make your decisions based on what makes me happy. You need to do what's best for you."

Tears pricked at the back of her eyes just knowing how hard it must have been for her dad to come to these realizations, let alone talk to her about them.

"Dad, I—"

"Life's too short, Dee." He leaned forward and took her hand in his. "You need to be happy. And if you're happy in Toronto, that's where you should be."

He said everything she'd wanted him to say. Deanna had to blink hard to keep her tears at bay. It's all she'd wanted from her dad: to give her permission to leave Cedar Springs. Not that she'd needed it. Not really. But the little girl in her had always wanted it. Had her ridiculous and childish plan really worked? She had to know. "Is this because of Marcus, Dad? Because if it—"

He stopped her with a shake of his head. "This is about you, Deanna. All I've ever wanted for you is for you to be happy. Are you happy?"

She opened her mouth to tell him that she couldn't be happy in Cedar Springs. That she needed the excitement of the big city and the emergency room to feel fulfilled. But she couldn't say those things. Because they were no longer true.

Being back in Cedar Springs had changed her. And it wasn't just Marcus, although she'd be lying if she said he wasn't part of it. He was. A huge part of it. But it was more than that. "I am happy, Dad."

"In Toronto?" He nodded and looked away.

Deanna squeezed her dad's hand so he looked back at her again. "No, Dad. Here. I'm happy here."

"What are you saying?"

She wasn't sure what she was saying. He'd basically just given her his blessing to leave Cedar Springs and his practice behind and go back to the big city. Everything she'd been working at since she'd come home. All she'd ever wanted was to get out of Cedar Springs and have a life somewhere else. But the irony was, her life was here.

"I'm saying, I don't want to leave." A smile crossed her face as she spoke and realized what she said was true. "I'm happy here. In Cedar Springs."

A tear slid down her father's cheek and it squeezed her heart. "I can't tell you what it means to hear you say that, Dee. But only if you're sure."

Deanna squeezed her eyes shut for a moment and let the last few months that she'd been back in town replay through her mind. She never thought she'd be satisfied with a small-town clinic, but helping people, and becoming part of their lives, was more satisfying than she could have guessed. The Slush Cup, the parties, her friends, Marcus. All of it. Her happiness had snuck up on her, but it was definitely there. She finally felt as if she belonged somewhere. She nodded. "I'm sure."

"And the boy?"

She almost laughed aloud at her dad's choice of words. "You mean Marcus?"

He nodded tersely.

"This has nothing to do with Marcus."

As she said the words, she realized they were true. With the taste of him still on her lips and the memory of him inside her, she knew there were feelings there. Yes. Definitely. But her decision to stay in Cedar Springs—it was hers and hers alone.

MARCUS DIDN'T EVEN TRY to be quiet as he slammed into the house. He couldn't even begin to process what had happened. How one woman could take him from indifferent, to angry, to heated passion so raw he couldn't control himself, to tenderness that threatened to consume him, he couldn't figure out. Deanna made him crazy. That was all he knew. It was all happening again. He'd done his best to stay distant. To keep their arrangement business only. But acting the role of her partner and not feeling anything was hard. Too hard.

Making love with Deanna—it had been risky and not just because they could have been caught if someone happened to stumble upon them. No, that was the least of his troubles. The real danger had been in risking his heart. Because being with her, he couldn't keep the two things separate. And it had felt so right. It would be too easy to let himself fall for her again, and the one thing he knew is that he wouldn't let it happen. He couldn't. There was no way he'd put himself through that type of hurt again. Once was enough, and she was capable of leaving him without a second glance. She'd done it before and she'd do it again. Especially considering that's what the whole deception was about: getting her out of Cedar Springs and away from him.

Not this time. He would not be left behind again. In the time it had taken to drop her off and drive up the mountain to Malcolm's home, he'd made up his mind. He refused to put himself through that again. She'd hurt him once. And that was enough.

Moving quickly, he tore into his bedroom and yanked his duffle bag out from under the bed. There was still a week until he'd have to leave for Europe for the filming, but he could use the time in Calgary to get his gear in order and reconnect with his sponsors.

With a new sense of determination, he moved quickly as he scooped his clothes out of the drawers and stuffed them into the bag. Koda whimpered at his feet and followed him around the room. No doubt the dog was confused, and it tugged at him. "Come here, buddy." He crouched on the floor; the puppy scrambled into his lap and licked his face. "I've gotta go for a bit, Koda. But you're going to stay here with Malcolm. He'll take good care of you and I'll be back for you, okay?" He couldn't be sure whether it was a lie or not, but he justified it because the dog wouldn't know either way. Koda licked him again, and he scratched the puppy's head before he let him go.

With renewed effort, Marcus went to the closet and grabbed what he could before he threw it on the bed.

"Think you could keep it down in here?" Malcolm appeared in his doorway, wearing nothing but a pair of boxer shorts. "I'm trying to sleep. What the...what are you doing?"

"I'm leaving." Marcus didn't spare his brother more than a glance. He couldn't. "I decided to rejoin the circuit and there's a movie being filmed in the Alps. I have to get moving if I'm—"

"Now?" Malcolm interrupted him. "It's like...ten thirty or something. Can't it wait until morning?"

"No. And what are you doing in bed at ten thirty?"

"Don't change the subject." Malcolm came into the room and bent down to pet the puppy. "What the hell is going on, Marcus?"

He should have known better than to try to fool his brother. Nobody knew him better than his twin. It was both a good thing and a full-blown annoyance.

"I told you," Marcus said. "I have to go. It's a good opportunity and I can't—"

"That's not what I meant and you know it." Malcolm scooped up the puppy and gave him a cuddle before he put him on the bed. "What's really going on? Weren't you out with Deanna tonight?"

Marcus shrugged. "It doesn't matter."

"Deanna doesn't matter?"

"You said yourself it wouldn't last." Marcus knew he was being cold, but it was the only way he could give himself distance. "You were right. Nothing ever lasts with me. She was only temporary. You knew it right from the beginning."

Malcolm shook his head. "No. I was wrong."

"You weren't." Marcus forced a laugh, but there was no humor in it. "That's the whole thing, brother. You were right."

"Deanna's different."

"No, she's not." The words tasted like acid on his tongue. She was different. She'd always been different. That was the whole problem.

"And what does she think about you leaving? It didn't go well, did it? That's why you're in such a hurry."

He shook his head.

"You didn't tell her?" Malcolm let out a long low whistle. "Nice, brother. You're just going to skip out on her and not even tell her? Just like you did with Kylie years ago. Real classy, Marcus. I thought you'd changed."

Marcus clenched his hands into fists. His brother thought he knew it all, but he didn't know anything. He didn't know it had been Deanna who had left him all those years ago. He'd left Kylie without a word because his own heart was broken and Kylie deserved better than him. She'd always deserved Malcolm. But this wasn't about Kylie. "You don't know what you're talking about, Malcolm."

"I know you leave when it gets hard, Marcus." Malcolm

moved so he stood between him and his bag. If his brother was looking for a fight, he was going to get it.

"You need to get out of my way, Malcolm. I'm not doing this right now."

"Yes you are."

That was it. Marcus stepped forward and swung. The punch didn't connect, but the one Malcolm fired back with did; Marcus staggered back from the blow before he caught himself. He regrouped and charged his brother. He connected hard and they toppled to the ground, fists flying. Some connected; most didn't. Finally, exhausting their anger, Marcus pulled himself away and grabbed his duffle off the bed.

"That's it, huh?" Malcolm pulled himself to his feet, but didn't come at him. "You're going to run anyway?"

"You don't know what you're talking about, Malcolm." Marcus shook his head. "It's over."

"Don't do it." Malcolm's voice lost some of its edge but Marcus wasn't ready to listen. "Seriously, Marcus. Don't do this. You're going to regret it."

Marcus paused for a moment in the door. He shook his head one more time and kept walking. What his brother didn't know was he already regretted it.

LOOKING AROUND THE STILLWATER RESTAURANT, Deanna couldn't help but be impressed. Pulling off a wedding shower in only a few days was a next to impossible task, but she had to hand it to Samantha because the place looked fantastic and she seemed to have pulled it off. The room was full of familiar faces, including the radiant bride-to-be, who looked even more radiant after her morning of spa services with her best friend that Deanna had booked for them.

Beth spotted her and made her way through the crowd to

give Deanna a big hug. "Thank you so much, Dee. Sam said you were such a big help pulling this together and the massages this morning...thank you."

Deanna beamed. "It was my pleasure. Really. I know you must be stressed with everything you have to do. I'm glad you enjoyed it."

"I really did." Beth picked up a canapé from a nearby table and popped it in her mouth. "Oh my goodness. These are so good. Jax is a miracle worker."

Deanna couldn't argue with that. Jax's food was amazing. She swore she probably had gained ten pounds just looking at it.

"You know," Beth said, "we're really going to miss you when you go back to Toronto. Do you really have to go back?"

Deanna smiled. She hadn't said anything, because she was still rolling it around in her head, and trying to process the idea of staying in Cedar Springs, but she'd woken up that morning feeling even better about her decision than when she'd gone to bed. It just felt right to stay in town. So what if she was giving up the excitement of the big city ER? What she was gaining was so much more. Besides, Cedar Springs was growing every day, and they were going to need another doctor, especially if her dad finally made good on his threat and retired. Yes, she'd percolated her decision in her head and she felt good about it. Really good. And even though she'd told her dad that Marcus wasn't the factor in her decision-making process, he was a factor. Whatever was happening between them, it might actually have a chance to be something this time.

"What's that little smile for?" Beth asked her.

She hadn't realized she was still grinning.

"Well, I wasn't going to say anything," Deanna said. "But, I've decided to stay in Cedar Springs."

"You're not going back to Toronto?" Beth's face lit up. "Really?"

"It's true."

Deanna laughed as Beth waved Samantha over.

"She's staying."

"You're staying?"

Deanna nodded at Sam. "It's true. I've decided to take over the practice. Well, assuming my dad wants to retire, anyway. He keeps saying he does. But..."

The women laughed and exchanged hugs again. "Well, this is great news," Sam said. "And we'll have to celebrate, soon. But right now, my friend, you are the star of this party. Come on, you have presents to open."

Beth groaned, but she had a smile on her face as she let Sam lead her away.

THE PARTY WAS a success and not only did Deanna enjoy herself with old friends and new ones, too, but there was a lightness to her that she hadn't felt in months. Maybe even years. Everything was coming together and the more people she spoke with, the better she felt about her decision to stay in Cedar Springs. Who knew, maybe she could even put down roots and start a family one day. The thought both excited her and freaked her out. Because when she closed her eyes and tried to picture that future, the only person who popped into her mind was Marcus. But she couldn't let her mind go that way. Not yet. Sure, just when she thought things between them were going well, they weren't. And then when she was ready to kill him, he went and made her love him again. _Love_. That was a strong word. No, she needed to stop thinking about it. At least for a bit.

Deanna turned her attention back to the party that had started to clear out. She'd see most of these same women at the wedding next weekend. Again, the idea that someone could get married so quickly boggled her mind, but then again it wasn't every day a friend was marrying a rock star with the need for secrecy. If anyone could pull it off, it would be Beth and Slade. Plus, it promised to be a fantastic wedding.

Just as she thought of the groom, he appeared, along with Malcolm, Jax, Rhys, Archer, Dylan, and Trent. Sam had said something about the guys going out fishing or some such thing as a makeshift bachelor party. Slade had insisted he didn't want a big production, so they'd kept it low-key. If they were all here, Marcus must be with them, too. Deanna tried to look casual as she scanned the crowd, but she couldn't see him.

"Hey." She turned to see Malcolm behind her with a plate loaded with cake and leftover canapés. "Good party. Kylie will be sorry she missed it."

Deanna flinched at the name. She hated the rift between them; she was going to have to do something about that and soon. Especially considering she would be staying in Cedar Springs. She didn't want it to be awkward between them. Not when they used to be such good friends. "Well, I guess it's too hard to get away every weekend, right?" Deanna smiled sympathetically. "And she'll be back for the wedding next weekend. That'll be good."

"It will be." Malcolm took a bite of cake. "I heard the good news. You're staying in Cedar Springs. That's great."

She didn't even try to hide her smile. "I am. It just feels right, you know?"

"I do know." Malcolm nodded. "That's how I felt when I came back here. There's no place quite like this town."

"I actually haven't even told Marcus yet," Deanna added, conscious that as far as everyone knew, they were still in their *fake relationship*. "I probably should tell him before he hears it through the grapevine. Is he with you guys?" She twisted her head around to see whether she could spot him yet. When she looked back at Malcolm, the smile had fallen off his face. "What? What's wrong?"

Before he even spoke, an icy fear crept through her. Something was wrong and she didn't need to hear it to know it.

"You don't know?" Malcolm said. "I was hoping maybe..."

"Obviously not." She wrapped her arms around her midsection, instinctively needing to hold herself together. "Tell me." Her voice shook. "What's going on, Malcolm?"

"I'm sorry, Deanna." He put his plate down and touched her arm. "Marcus is gone."

Chapter Thirteen

EVERYTHING WAS IN SLOW MOTION. Her whole week had been in slow motion, as if she looked at herself from the outside. Yet everything else around Deanna moved at warp speed. The whole town had been in a frenzy over the wedding, and Deanna knew she should be caught up in it, too. It would probably take her mind off everything else, but she couldn't seem to muster any energy for it. Every step felt as if she were dragging her feet through mud and all she wanted to do was sleep.

She'd only felt like this one other time in her life. Only the roles had been reversed. She'd been the one who'd done the leaving. It didn't feel any better to be the one who was left behind. In fact, she was pretty sure it felt worse.

He'd left without a note, or a phone call. Not even a text. And no, they didn't have a relationship in the legitimate sense, but they did. He'd kissed her and held her and...it had been real. There was no doubt in her mind that it had been real. She wasn't naive enough to think that sex always meant love, but with Marcus, it was more than sex. It always had been.

It didn't matter, though, because she'd meant it when she'd said she made her decision to stay in Cedar Springs without regard to Marcus. It was true. She wanted to stay and that didn't change because her heart was broken. Besides, she only had herself to blame for that.

She looked in the mirror and adjusted the straps of her dress again. She'd picked out a fitted sundress for the wedding that showcased her cleavage without revealing too much. The blues in the print made her eyes sparkle. Well, they usually made them sparkle. When she stared into the mirror, Deanna couldn't see much life in them at all. But she'd do her best to put on a good show. It was a wedding, after all. A celebration of love for her friends. She wasn't going to do anything to ruin that.

Before she left the house, she tucked her oversized sunglasses into her purse just in case she didn't do as good of a job pretending as she hoped to.

DEANNA COULDN'T HAVE IMAGINED A MORE romantic location for a wedding ceremony than the Springs resort and given that it was where Slade and Beth met for the first time, it was the perfect choice for the wedding. There were so many beautiful locations, but the couple had chosen to have their ceremony in the main hall with the large glass windows that showcased the mountains outside as a backdrop. It was simple and stunning. A small altar was the centerpiece, with rows of chairs set up in a fan to give guests the best view. The water features of the Springs bubbled and flowed, and the addition of huge arrangements of hydrangeas and white roses on every surface gave the whole space an even more romantic air.

She stopped and took it all in. It was perfect. A wave of sadness washed through her, but Deanna bit back her tears.

She would not, could not fall apart. Not today. A wedding was a celebration of love and she would not be the person who brought even the slightest twinge of sadness to the day.

No. She could hold it together for a few hours.

"Deanna?"

She turned and was immediately pulled into Cynthia's arms for a hug. The touch almost was her undoing, but she maintained her composure. "How are you?" Deanna stepped back and looked at her friend. She was absolutely glowing with her pregnancy. "You look amazing. Are you feeling well?"

"I am." She smiled and her hand floated to her swelling belly. "I almost feel bad that I feel so good. Does that make sense?"

"It does." Deanna laughed. "But don't feel bad. Everyone experiences pregnancy differently. There is no right way. So enjoy it."

A flash of movement caught their attention. Seth waved in Cynthia's direction and held up two fingers. "I think he has seats for us," Cynthia said. "Why don't you come sit with us?"

It was a generous offer and one that Deanna knew came from a place of genuine friendship, but the day was going to be hard enough. She wasn't sure she could sit next to a happy couple and watch another couple get married without totally breaking down. It would be too much. She shook her head. "You know what? I think I'm going to hang out back here. I like to be one of the first to see the bride when she comes in." It wasn't a total lie but Deanna knew there was no way she could sit among happy couples watching the ultimate commitment of love and hold herself together. That was not going to happen. It was definitely best if she hung out at the back.

Cynthia looked at her and for a moment Deanna was afraid she was going to insist. Instead, her friend pulled her into another hug. "I'm so sorry to hear about you and Marcus," she whispered in her ear. "I just don't understand it. I saw the way he looked at you and that doesn't come along every day."

Deanna knew Cynthia wasn't trying to make her cry, but her words hit her harder than her friend could have known. If Cynthia knew that all of that between them was just an act, she'd feel differently. Probably. Even though Deanna knew herself it had all been an act, wasn't she having the most trouble of all, trying to process how he could have left her?

She forced a smile. "It looks like they want us to sit." Deanna gestured to the usher, who was trying to get everyone to take their seats. It was a very welcome distraction and Cynthia headed to her seat, leaving Deanna alone.

The back row was mostly empty, so Deanna took a spot close to the end where she could slip away if she needed to and waited patiently, her eyes fixed ahead of her to avoid eye contact with anyone.

Beautiful music floated through the air. Slade and a man Deanna had never seen before but who looked an awful lot like Slade himself came to stand at the altar. She knew Samantha had said something about one of Slade's cousins coming in for the ceremony, but they could have been brothers for all the similarities they shared. Deanna turned to look behind her as an older woman dressed in a flowing robe-like dress made her way down the aisle. She almost pranced and an energy came off her that made Deanna smile. She'd heard that a friend of Slade's, Mona Sheridan, was going to perform the ceremony and that she was quite the character. From what Deanna had heard, Mona played a bit of a role in Slade and Beth connecting. Or at least, she liked to think she did. Deanna's mood lightened considerably as she watched the older woman walk down the aisle, waving and blowing kisses to people in the crowd. When she got to the front of the room, she gave Slade a hug and took her place next to him.

The music shifted and Deanna turned again to see Jules,

Beth's daughter, looking impossibly grown up in a shimmery blue dress. She carried a bouquet of white roses with blue blossoms of hydrangea tucked among them. Deanna had only seen her a handful of times since being back in town, but she was definitely not the little girl Dee remembered. Time moved so quickly. It seemed almost impossible that Jules could be a teenager already. She beamed up at Slade as she approached the front and Slade bent to give her a kiss on the cheek and a big hug before he held her hand.

Samantha was the next down the aisle, wearing an equally gorgeous dress. Her hair was piled on her head in a simple and sexy updo. There was a quiet whistle from a few rows down, and Samantha blushed and shot Trent a look. Deanna felt a twinge of jealousy at the desire the two of them felt for each other, but quickly focused again as the music shifted once more. The crowd rose to their feet as Beth came into view. Her arm was looped through Rhys Anderson's. Dressed in his ceremonial police uniform, he looked both proud and emotional as he walked with his childhood sweetheart and close friend. Rhys and Beth had always shared a connection that most didn't understand, but they'd never been meant to be together. It made Deanna's heart swell to watch them together now, coming full circle.

Beth looked absolutely stunning in her simple floor-length gown. When she passed Deanna, she could see the plunging back and beadwork down the backside of the dress. Just the right amount of sexy and classy, just like Beth herself. She was one of the most beautiful brides Deanna had ever seen. Her heart was full and tears pricked at her eyes as she watched them make their way down the aisle. As the crowd sat, Deanna dug into her purse for a tissue to dab at her eyes. She was never going to get through the day without a few tears. At least she could pass them off as typical wedding happy tears.

She wasn't looking, so she didn't see the man who slid into the seat next to her until he bumped her arm and knocked her purse to the floor. "What the—"

"I'm sorry, I—"

Without bothering to see who the inconsiderate, clumsy man was, Deanna bent and quickly pulled the contents of her purse together before the ceremony could begin.

"Let me help you."

Deanna shoved her things into her bag and sat up. "I've got —" The words died on her lips as she stared into a set of eyes she never thought she'd see again.

MARCUS PACED the terminal of the Calgary airport for what had to be the dozenth time. All week he'd been preparing for his trip to Europe, which mostly meant securing a new board and picking up some new gear to replace the stuff he'd left at Malcolm's. He'd left in such a hurry he hadn't bothered to grab everything, but there was no way he was going back. Not after that exit.

He'd spent the majority of the last few days consumed by thoughts of Deanna: The way she'd looked at him. The way her mouth tasted on his. The way she moved when he was inside her. But mostly the way the smile would have fallen from her face when she heard that he'd left and hadn't said goodbye. That was the thought that haunted him all week as he'd waited for his departure date to Zurich.

She hadn't called or texted him at all, but she had to know he was gone. Malcolm would have made it a point to tell her. Not to hurt her, but more to protect her. Marcus hadn't really expected her to reach out to him, but every time he checked his phone and saw there were still no messages, something inside him broke a little bit. Mostly it was the guilt. He'd done to her exactly what she'd done to him years ago. And he knew first-hand how badly that hurt.

Only this time it was different. Because they weren't kids anymore, with other commitments and expectations that had been put upon them. They weren't sneaking around this time. Their relationship was totally out in the open. But it hadn't been real.

He ran his hands through his hair and tugged at the roots. That was bullshit and he knew it.

It *had* been real.

And he'd walked away.

A voice over the loudspeaker announced his flight had started pre-boarding.

He was running out of time.

Marcus dug out his phone and looked at the blank screen again. He didn't know what he'd been expecting. Deanna was too proud to text him. Or too stubborn. Either way, he might be a little disappointed not to see her name there, but he wasn't surprised. However, he was surprised that he hadn't heard from his brother. They'd had their differences over the years, but no matter what they'd done, they'd never stopped talking. They were brothers. Twin brothers. Whatever Malcolm thought about the choices Marcus was making, he still should have reached out. Said good-bye. Whatever.

The voice over the speaker announced they were boarding group one.

This was it. In a few minutes, he'd get on the plane and be on his way to Europe and the opportunity to once again get away from Cedar Springs and the woman who, whether he liked it or not, had his heart.

Only this time, Marcus knew that once he left, there'd be no going back. That was the thought that had sat heavy with him all week.

He picked up his duffle and pulled his ticket from his pocket. He'd already checked his snowboard and another bag of gear. He was committed to the flight.

"We will now begin our final boarding call for flight 1254 to Zurich."

The voice jarred him. *Final call.*

This was it.

He adjusted the strap of his bag and moved slowly to the gate.

A ten-hour flight and he'd be an ocean away. A world away.

"Your ticket, sir."

Marcus froze and looked at the paper in his hand. Seat 10A. A window seat.

Deanna. Did she like the window seat or the aisle?

"Sir?"

Marcus shook his head in an effort to clear it.

"Your ticket, sir. I need to scan it before you can board."

Marcus swallowed hard and tried one more time to push all the images of Deanna out of his mind. He glanced over his shoulder at the empty concourse and then back to the flight attendant, who looked less than impressed as she waited for him. With a sigh, he raised his arm and handed her the ticket.

THE CEREMONY WAS both touching and lighthearted. Just like the couple themselves. It was easy to see how much in love they were and the love that Slade had for Jules was evident as they participated in a commitment ceremony of their own. He pledged to always be there for her, to care for her, love her and protect her; Jules, with a very serious expression on her face, promised in return to love him and take him as her father, to share good times, and hard ones, and weather whatever storm they came across, together.

And then it was Beth's turn.

As the crowd wiped their tears and composed themselves, Mona cleared her throat and clasped her hands together in front of her. "It is my honor to be here today, with Simon and Beth." Deanna smiled at the use of Slade's given name. "I was there in the beginning when these two lovebirds finally came to see the future in each other's eyes, and it's only fitting that I be the one to unite them in their commitment." There were a few chuckles and Mona grinned. "There is so much more to a loving, committed relationship than what one simply sees," Mona began. "It is about cultivating patience, understanding, flexibility, and a sense of humor. Love is having the capacity to forgive each other and forget the minor transgressions that we as humans make from time to time. Love is not only about finding the right partner, but *being* the right partner. We are all gathered here today with Simon and Beth to celebrate that love and witness the entwining of two beautiful hearts and spirits into one. After today, you will no longer be separate entities, but united in a companionship of strength and unity. By standing here today, you are agreeing to share strength, responsibilities, and love."

Beth and Slade both nodded slightly and Beth dabbed at her eyes with a tissue.

Mona smiled and touched Beth's arm before she turned to the groom. "Simon. Do you have a few words to share with your bride?"

He nodded and turned to Beth, taking both her hands in his. "Beth, I love you. I love you for what you are and what I am when I'm with you. You are my partner and my one true love. I will always honor you, respect you, and treat you like the goddess you are." A few twitters and giggles came from the crowd, but he didn't seem to notice anything but the woman in front of him. "I vow to love you, honor, and respect you until the day I draw my last breath."

Mona nodded sagely, a satisfied smile on her face. She waited for Beth to compose herself and wipe her tears before she gestured for Slade to put the ring on her finger. When he had finished, Mona looked to Beth. "Do you have a few words to share with your groom?"

Beth nodded and with a quiet, shaking voice, she said, "Slade, from the moment I met you, I knew my life would be forever changed. I love you for the man you are both to me and my daughter. You make me want to be a better version of myself every day. I vow to laugh with you, love you, and fight with you through the hard times. From this day forward, you are my heart, my dreams, my life."

She got through her vows and before Mona told her to, Beth placed the ring she had on Slade's finger. As soon as it was in place, he pulled her into his arms and kissed her thoroughly.

Mona laughed and threw up her arms. "Well, I suppose it doesn't need to be said, but...you may now seal your union with a kiss."

The crowd erupted into cheers and hollers of appreciation.

"He certainly knows how it's done."

Deanna turned to the man who'd been sitting somewhat awkwardly next to her throughout the entire ceremony. To be fair, it wasn't him who was awkward; it was her. She hadn't seen Ian McCormick in years. Not since the summer he'd come to town with his family and taken her virginity. They were young, dumb, and reckless, and beyond that one night, they didn't mean anything to each other. But Deanna never thought she'd actually see him again. Even when Sam told her he would be returning, she hadn't thought about what it would mean to sit next to him again after so many years. Not really, anyway.

"He loves her," she said, and the tears she'd been fighting burned her inner eyes again. "It's sweet."

Ian nodded. "It is."

They all stood as Mona announced the couple and Beth and Slade, with Jules next to them, skipped down the aisle. Once the wedding party was gone, Ian grabbed her arm and held her eyes. "It's good to see you again, Deanna. It's been a long time."

She nodded.

"You look great."

"Thank you."

"I bet you're wondering why I'm back?"

She shrugged.

"Well, maybe we can talk about it sometime over drinks."

If he was flirting with her, she didn't have the energy to realize it. She nodded and mustered a smile, which quickly faded as she saw Kylie behind him. She hadn't dealt with that situation. Not since their blow-up in the kitchen, and Deanna knew she owed her friend an apology. A big one.

"That would be nice," she said to Ian. "But if you'll excuse me, I have to..."

He turned and saw Kylie waiting to talk to her. "Maybe you'll save me a dance later?"

"Sure." She didn't really mean it, but she needed to talk to Kylie, and Ian didn't seem to be in a hurry to go anywhere. Her agreement seemed to be good enough for him and he slipped away.

"Was that Ian McCormick?" Kylie stepped up. "He looks...well, he looks good."

Deanna smiled at Kylie's choice of words, because Ian McCormick did look good. The last time they'd seen him he was a cocky, overconfident teenager who knew exactly how good-looking he was. He was still way too good-looking than was probably healthy for one man, but Deanna's first impressions of Ian was that he seemed softer somehow, less arrogant. It would definitely be interesting having the McCormicks around again. Not that she cared much either way. Not where Ian was concerned. That was old news. Really old news. "He does," she agreed with Kylie. "I didn't expect to see him here."

"I don't think he was invited, to be honest," Kylie said. "But then again, some who were invited didn't bother showing up."

There was no doubt who Kylie referred to, but Deanna didn't take the bait. She was tired of fighting and lying and...she was just tired.

"Look, Kylie. I'm really—"

"Don't apologize, okay?"

"But I need to."

"No you don't." Kylie reached out her hand to Deanna's arm and the gentle touch shattered something inside her. The tears she'd been trying to hold back slipped down her cheek. "It's okay," Kylie said.

"No." Dee shook her head. "It's really not. I've made such a mess of everything and now..."

"He's gone."

Deanna nodded. "And he didn't even say good-bye." She realized as she spoke that it was exactly what she'd done to him all those years ago.

Kylie laughed a little, but it wasn't a menacing sound. "You two definitely have a habit of doing that to each other, don't you?"

Deanna nodded and laughed a little through her tears. "We do."

"You really love him, don't you?"

It was her chance to tell Kylie the truth about the lie, and the deception they'd been playing on everyone, but she couldn't. Even knowing it was all over, she couldn't bring herself to diminish their connection in that way. "I do."

Kylie's smile was soft. "I know." She pulled Deanna into a hug and right there in the middle of a crowd of her family and friends, Deanna let herself cry.

Chapter Fourteen

THE WEDDING DINNER had been a feast of steak and shrimp and some fancy side dishes that Deanna had never heard of before, but Jax Carver had pulled out all the stops for his friend's special day. By the time the plates were cleared and the dance floor was made ready, everyone was stuffed and more than ready to get up and get moving.

Everything about the wedding had been amazing and Deanna marveled over how they possibly could have pulled it off in only two short weeks. But when cost wasn't a consideration, there were all kinds of ways to make things happen. Besides, Beth and Slade had a host of excellent friends and family who'd all worked together to make their day so wonderful.

In fact, she'd been having such a good time, Deanna had allowed herself to forget about Marcus and the fact that he was likely somewhere over the Atlantic Ocean by now, on his way to Europe and far away from her.

"Hey there."

She didn't need to look over to know Ian stood next to her. He'd watched her all night from across the room, smiling and waving, and she'd done her best to avoid him. Especially considering he was only giving her that kind of attention because of their history, no matter how short it had been. He was new to town again, and he needed a familiar face to latch onto. That was all. But at the same time, he was a welcome distraction from her heartache and if she could just get through the rest of the night, Deanna knew she'd be okay.

"Hey yourself." She didn't turn to look at him. "How did you manage an invitation to this anyway?"

"Straight to the hard questions." He laughed. "Okay, I'll play along. I didn't. Samantha mentioned it and I just decided to come. I didn't have anything else going on anyway."

Deanna turned to him then and raised her eyebrow. "Really? That's ballsy."

He shrugged and laughed. "Well, I figured I better start to get to know people since I'm back now. And I liked spending time with you back in the day."

She turned her attention back to the dance floor. "Things were different then."

"How so?"

It was her turn to shrug.

"Are you with someone?"

Ian always could cut right to the chase. "Yes." It was a reflex answer. One she quickly amended. "No. Well, not really."

"Which is it?"

Her eyes swam with tears when she looked at him.

"Ah." The touch of his hand on her shoulder was soft and sensitive and just what she needed. "I understand."

And she knew he did. She nodded slightly. "Thank you."

"I know that kind of heartache," Ian said. "And I know the best thing for it."

She laughed and tried to pull away from him. "If you say what I think you're going to say, then I'm outta here."

It was Ian's turn to laugh. "Well," he wiggled his eyebrows at her, "I wasn't going to say that, but it helps too. What I was going to say was..." He took her by the hand and tugged gently. "Dancing. Come on. Nothing cures a broken heart like getting down on the dance floor." She couldn't argue with that and besides, it was better than standing around and watching everyone else have fun, so Deanna let him lead her onto the dance floor.

Ian had always been smooth and it was no surprise that he was a good dancer. He was a confident lead and spun her around until she was laughing and smiling, having a great time and almost had totally forgotten about Marcus. Almost.

When a slow song came on, Deanna tried to wriggle away, but Ian quickly and smoothly wrapped his arm around her and pulled her close. "Don't run away. I told you, dancing is good for your soul. It'll make you feel better."

Deanna couldn't be sure how letting another man hold her in his arms could possibly make her feel better, but to her surprise, the movement helped. As if all the sad feelings flowed into her through the rhythm of the music and then right back out again, leaving her feeling oddly...better. "It's actually working," she said when he asked how she was feeling.

"Good." He slid his hand up her back, in a move that should have felt intimate, but didn't. "Now rest your head on my shoulder. It helps, I promise." She looked up at him with narrowed eyes, but he only laughed. "I swear, totally innocent."

Deanna didn't see how it could hurt, so she let her head rest on his shoulder as he continued to hold her and sway to the rhythm of the music. It was a romantic love song that she'd heard a million times but never bothered to pay attention to the lyrics before. She felt tears fill her eyes and knew she was likely leaving a damp spot on his shirt, but she didn't care. Ian made a comforting sound and rubbed her back, letting her cry in privacy as they moved slowly around the floor.

MARCUS HAD DRIVEN like a bat out of hell, pushing the very boundaries of safety on the curvy mountain roads in the rental car he'd managed to secure last minute, but he didn't care. He'd handed his ticket to the flight attendant, but as soon as he heard the beep as she scanned it into the system, something clicked. Without a word of explanation to the woman who still held his ticket, he'd turned and sprinted through the concourse, out past security and to the closest rental car counter he could find.

That was just over three hours ago, and he was finally coming into Cedar Springs. He'd made brilliant time and was lucky, damn lucky, he hadn't encountered the sheriff or any wildlife, for that matter. He wasn't in the mood to be slowed down in any way. He needed to get to Deanna.

He navigated his car through the main street and up the twisty mountain road to the Springs resort. He'd have to beg Slade and Beth forgiveness for missing their wedding, but he couldn't think of how he would deal with that. Not yet. His only thought was on Deanna. He pulled up to the front door and left the car in the loading zone before he sprinted through the halls to the banquet room. He passed a few people he recognized as he went, but didn't bother to say hi or acknowledge their greetings. He had laser focus.

He slipped into the room and immediately scanned the room for her. For the first time, he had a flash of doubt. He'd assumed she'd be there. But what if she wasn't? What if she'd gone home already? Or just not come at all? What if she'd gone back to Toronto?

Marcus's eyes landed on Beth, who looked radiant on Slade's arm. The perfect happy couple. He quickly looked away and saw Samantha with Kylie, Trent, and of course, Malcolm. As if his brother had twin radar, Malcolm's head turned and their eyes locked. Marcus didn't see the look of shock or surprise he'd expected from his brother. Instead, Malcolm shook his head a little and let out what even from a distance looked like a big sigh. Marcus tried to ask him with his eyes were Deanna might be, but Malcolm looked away.

Fine. He'd find her on his—

There.

Deanna.

Dancing with...oh hell no.

Before he could stop to process anything, Marcus pushed his way through the crowd and onto the dance floor. He grabbed the man and yanked him away from his woman before he slipped his arm around Deanna and pulled her to him.

"What the—"

"Marcus!"

"Do you know him?"

"Damn right she does." Marcus puffed up his chest. "I'm her boyfriend."

"You are not." Deanna struggled in his arm, trying to get away from him, but he wouldn't release her. If he had his way, he'd never let her go again. "Marcus. Stop it."

"I think you should take your hands off her."

By this time, they'd attracted bit of a crowd and Marcus looked up to see Slade watching him. Reluctantly, he let his arm slide away and the moment it did, Deanna turned and ran off the dance floor.

"What the hell is your problem, man?" The man who'd had his arms around Deanna stood inches away from him and it took all Marcus's self-control not to take a swing at him.

"I have to go." He wasn't going to waste his time engaging this asshole, not when Deanna was getting away. He had his priorities. And she was the only one on that list.

He heard his name being called behind him, but he didn't

stop or slow down. Marcus made it out into the corridor just in time to see Deanna disappear through a door out to the gardens.

"Deanna!"

Either she hadn't heard him or she ignored him. He hoped like hell it was the former as he went after her.

The night air was cool; it was still spring in the mountains, after all. Although the days could be hot, the nights were still chilly and it wasn't unusual to get a frost at this time of year. "Deanna?"

He heard a noise that sounded suspiciously like a sob and headed in that direction. She stood with her arms wrapped tightly around herself and stared into the darkness. "Deanna?" His voice was softer this time.

"Go away, Marcus."

"You know I won't."

She spun so quickly he had to take a step back. "I *don't* know that, actually. Because isn't that what you *just* did?" Tears streamed down her face and it physically hurt him to see her in pain and know that he'd caused it. "Marcus, you left. So could you just do me a favor and do it again?" She turned again so her back was to him. "Go away."

"No."

"Marcus." The sigh that escaped her lips deflated her shoulders and she fell in on herself a little. "Please. I just can't."

"You don't really want me to leave, Dee."

She was silent for a second and the urge to grab her and turn her in to his arms was so strong it threatened to consume him. She shook her head, but didn't answer him.

"You don't want me to go, Dee. Unless..." The image of her dancing with that man flashed in his head. They looked pretty damn cozy. Jealousy flashed through him like white light. "That guy. Is he—"

"Stop it." She turned again. "Please. Just stop. He's an old friend. Nothing more and you know it."

He did and shame for even insinuating there was something more filled him. "I'm sorry, but you make me—"

"What, Marcus? I make you what? Want to leave?" Tears flowed down her face and she made no move to wipe them away. "Want to run away as soon as it starts getting too real?"

"No." His answer was as honest as it could be. "You make me crazy, Dee. You always have." He grabbed her hand and squeezed it tight. She shook like a leaf. From the cold or from whatever it was that was going on with them, he didn't know, but he held her fast, resisting the urge to pull her into him. "I left because I was...." He couldn't finish the thought. Up until that moment, he hadn't fully understood why he'd left. All he knew was he had to get away. And once he was gone, he needed to be with her.

"What, Marcus?" There was so much hope and expectation in her eyes. "What was it?"

That was the moment. It was all in front of him. All he had to do was be honest. He took a deep breath and exhaled slowly. "I left because I couldn't let it happen again."

"What?"

"I couldn't let you leave me again, Dee." He took her other hand in his and held her fast. "All the time we were together, pretending to be something we weren't—at some point, it became more. A lot more. And then all I could think of was that you were going to leave again, Dee. Just the way you left me the first time."

"I didn't—"

"You did and it killed me." Marcus had a moment where he thought maybe, just maybe, he should temper what he was saying. But he shoved it aside. He was being honest. Totally and completely honest. It was something he should have done a long time ago and he knew in his heart it was the only way he had a hope in hell to be with her. "I was so scared you'd hurt me again. Because Deanna, you have my heart. All of it. And you always have. There's never been another woman like you and there never will be." Her tears came faster and harder, running unchecked down her cheeks. "Why are you crying?"

She smiled through her tears and shook her head. "Because I'm not running anymore."

"What?"

Her smile was so sweet and so full of emotion, Marcus thought it might tear out his heart. "I'm not going anywhere, Marcus. I'm staying right here in Cedar Springs."

"You are?"

She nodded and laughed a little, even though there was nothing funny about anything. "I am. That last night we were together, I told my father the truth and told him I wanted to stay."

"Because of..."

"Because of me. I need to do this. I *want* to do it." She shrugged and even in the dim light, he could see her blush. "But it would have been pretty nice if you were here, too."

"And what if I told you I was staying?"

"What?"

"Would that change things?"

"For me or for you?"

He stared into her eyes for a moment, waiting to hear what she might say. But he couldn't wait. "Screw it." No longer caring about the answer she might or might not give, he pulled her into his arms and put his lips on hers. She tasted sweet, like sugar and champagne, and he drank her up until she melted into his arms and kissed him back with just as much heat as he was giving.

"This changes everything," he said when he finally pulled away. "I'm not going anywhere."

"But your circuit. The movie."

"I don't care."

She shook her head, and tried to look away. "Of course you care. Marcus, it's your career."

He smiled and touched her nose gently with his. "It *was* my career. Maybe it's time for a change. I've been working on some new snowboard designs and have some savings tucked away. Maybe it's time for the *King of the Board* to try his hand at designing those boards."

"Really?"

He nodded. "Especially if it keeps me here in Cedar Springs. With you. Because, Deanna Gordon, now that I have you in my arms again, I'm never going to let you go. I have loved you from the moment I met you."

"Marcus, I—"

"Love me, too." He'd taken a leap, and no matter what she said, he wouldn't regret it. "I know it's true. I'm done with games and pretending. I just want to be real with you, Dee, and—"

"I love you, Marcus Stone." She laughed and the sound filled him up. "I always have and it's long past time you knew it."

Summer is coming and there's a new family in town. The McCormick's are back and Ian McCormick is already making a big impression. But not everyone is happy to see his familiar face. Read on to see how the McCormicks are going to rock Cedar Springs with an exclusive excerpt of Love in the Moment right after this ——>

If you're enjoying the friends of Cedar Springs, you will absolutely fall in love with the four best friends

of Timber Creek! Emotion packed stories of second chances, will make you believe in love again! One click When We Left for FREE right now!

And if you like a sweeter small town romance, don't miss falling in love with the best selling Castle Mountain Lodge Series! Download Unexpected Gifts NOW!

I appreciate you helping me spread the word about the books you love! Reviews help readers discover their next favorite read! Please leave a review on your favorite book retailer!

Don't forget to join my mailing list where you'll be the first to hear about new stories, sales and promotions and giveaways!
You can join me here —>
https://elenaaitken.com/newsletter/

Love in the Moment

WALKING along the lakefront in front of his old family cabin, Ian McCormick was hit by a flood of different feelings. He'd had so many good memories of his summers spent there as kids. Every year, his mother would load the four of them in the van and they'd make the drive out to the lake, where they'd spend the next two and a half months playing, swimming, getting into trouble, and basically having the best summer any kid could ask for. His father would come out for a few weeks in July and the occasional weekend here and there, but mostly it was just the boys and their mother.

It had been perfect.

Until the truth came out.

The perfect family the McCormicks presented themselves to be were anything but. He was in his first year of college when his father had finally announced he was leaving their mother, and them, for his other family.

His. Other. Family.

For over fifteen years, his father had led a double life and had another woman, and worse, children. Two girls. His sisters.

Ian had made a vow that day that he would have nothing to do with them.

He made his way to the waterline and threw a rock as far out as he could. He watched the ripples fan out and dissipate as they went. *The ripple effect.* He laughed at the irony. That's exactly what his father's actions had caused. He'd been successful for years in keeping his vow to distance himself from his *other family*. Two of his younger brothers, Declan and Cal, who were still in junior high school when everything went down, had been involved with their half-sisters Chelsea and Amber and even gotten to know them. They were closer in age, all four of them had been somewhere between sixteen and thirteen, and much to Ian's annoyance, they'd become sort of friends. It was harder for Ian, and Mitch, his other brother. They didn't look at it the same way. They couldn't see past the hurt on their mother's face. How she had to start over and work two jobs to scrape by while her father went on to happily live a different life. It was beyond Ian how he could have done that to her.

He didn't blame Chelsea and Amber. Not really.

But it didn't make it any easier to be around them. Which is why he had no idea why he'd agreed when Declan had called him and asked him for a favor. Not just a favor, but a total sacrifice.

A few months earlier, Ian told his brothers that he'd planned to return to Cedar Springs to open up the old house for the summer and check out the business opportunities in town. Recently there'd been a resurgence of business in town and Ian was always one to jump on a good investment. But when Declan had called to ask him to please let Chelsea, the youngest of the two girls, to spend the summer with him, Ian had been expecting anything but that. She was only twenty-two and according to Declan, a good girl, but lost and confused.

She needed to get out of the city and away from the influences that were steering her down the wrong path.

"Whatever." He threw another rock. "Not. My. Problem." Ian kicked a pile of rocks and scared some ducks that nested nearby. He immediately felt guilty. Just the way he had when Declan told him how rough it had been for Chelsea. Apparently she had a lot of pent-up anger at both her parents and being around them was only feeding her rage.

"Join the club." Ian laughed and shook his head.

In the end, he'd agreed.

And if he didn't hurry, he'd be late to pick her up. She was set to come in on the four o'clock bus, and Ian planned to take her straight over to meet Samantha. He'd secured her a job at the Grizzly Paw, because he'd be damned if she was going to lie around in the sun all summer and not pull her weight. Leaving the beach behind, he jumped into his Jeep and set into town. The row of old log homes that used to be full of activity and bustle for the summer were still mostly locked up. That would change. It was still early. But in a few months, when school got out for summer, his old summer neighborhood would be full of life again. It surprised him how much he was looking forward to it.

The bus had just pulled up when Ian arrived. He realized he had no real idea what Chelsea looked like beyond a few old pictures he'd reluctantly looked at years earlier; he probably hadn't seen a picture of her in the last few years. He scanned the crowd. There were a few elderly women who probably had been in the city visiting children and grandchildren, a few couples and then—Chelsea.

He strode through the small crowd and bent to pick up her bag before she could get it. He might not be happy about the situation, but he was still a gentleman. His hand locked around the handle of the duffle at the same time hers did. "I got it."

"What the—" She whipped the bag away from him hard

and fast with a strength that surprised him. "Get your hands off my stuff!"

"Whoa." Ian dropped the bag and held his hands up. "Chelsea, I'm your—"

"My name is not Chelsea." The woman, who now that he had a chance to look at her properly, had actually no family resemblance to him, glared at him.

"I'm sorry, I—"

"Thought that maybe you could just steal my things because I'm a woman traveling on my own." The woman stood tall and although she tried to appear tough, she likely hadn't accounted for the shaking of her hands as she held fast onto her duffle and tried to keep the giant tote bag she had over her shoulder from sliding off. Ian tried not to smile at her bravado, but there was something about her; he couldn't help it. "Oh," she said, her words pointed. "I suppose you think this is funny now? You would."

"I would?" He shook his head. "I don't. I assure you, I didn't mean to offend you. I thought you were—"

"Ian?"

He turned to see Chelsea—the actual Chelsea, he could see right away, because like it or not, there was definitely a strong McCormick family resemblance. "Chelsea?"

She shrugged and gave him a weak smile. She had one small duffle bag at her feet, and nothing more besides a purse over her thin body.

He hesitated for a moment, not knowing whether he was supposed to go to her, hug her or shake her hand. In the end, she came to him and smiled before she tucked her hands in her back pockets. *Good.* If she wasn't the hugging type, that would probably make things easier. "Well, it's good to...meet you, I guess."

"Yeah," he said lamely. "It's nice to finally meet you." His words sounded hollow, and he instantly regretted them. It wasn't her fault their father was an ass. "Should be a fun summer," he added quickly and immediately regretted it because it sounded even lamer. "Let's get going."

He picked up her bag, which was even lighter than it looked. He gave her a questioning glance, but she didn't look at him. "I'm just parked over here." He pointed to his Jeep. Before he walked away, he turned to apologize one more time to the woman he'd somehow inadvertently offended, but she was gone.

A twinge of regret he couldn't explain flared in his gut.

He would have liked to apologize again, maybe even learn her name.

Ian shook his head, clearing any ideas before they could take root. He didn't need any other complications. He headed toward the Jeep, where Chelsea was already settled in, tapping something on her phone. No doubt he already had his hands full. He had a feeling it was going to be a very interesting summer.

Who was the woman at the bus stop? And what was it about her that had Ian looking twice? Find out in Love in the Moment, NOW!

About the Author

Elena Aitken is a USA Today Bestselling Author of more than forty romance and women's fiction novels. Living a stone's throw from the Rocky Mountains with her teenager twins, their two cats and a goofy rescue dog, Elena escapes into the mountains whenever life allows. She can often be found with her toes in the lake and a glass of wine in her hand, dreaming up her next book and working on her own happily ever after with her very own mountain man.

To learn more about Elena:
www.elenaaitken.com
elena@elenaaitken.com

Acknowledgments

With every book I write, I learn so much, in so many ways. Writing Summit of Passion was a little different for me because nothing went according to schedule. Sometimes life happens, and factors out of your control, make it difficult. The most important thing I learned during this process was that I'm a very lucky woman. I am surrounded by amazing people, many of whom helped make this book in particular, a reality, not to mention they kept me sane and lifted me up in the process.

A huge thank you to the most amazing assistant Jennifer Wood. I could not have made it through the last few months without you. Thank you for picking up all the balls I kept dropping and keeping everything running so smoothly. You are amazing.

Major thank you to my editor Faith Williams who didn't even blink when I told her about my crazy deadlines. She just made it happen because she is simply awesome!

A very big hug and thank you to my children who are always so understanding about what Mom does, and how sometimes dinner isn't made on time or I have to close the door on my office. You're both fantastic children and I'm so proud of you.

And of course the biggest thank you to my readers. It is only because of YOU that I can do what I do everyday. Words cannot express how grateful I am that you choose to pick my books up and fall in love with the characters as much as I do. I wish I could give every single one of you a big hug! A special squishy hug to all the members of my street team who have given my ideas, inspiration and encouragement. I love you ladies!

Thank you!

Summit of Passion: The Springs, 7

Copyright © 2015 by Elena Aitken